MISSION: ASSASSINATION

Suddenly Bandit sprang into the air in stark terror.

Renegade!

There was a simultaneous flash of movement from among the rocks beside him. Varn went down, flinging himself forward and to the left, but even as he moved, a blaster discharged.

He was a dead man! No one could miss at that range . . .

STAR COMMANDOS

FIRE PLANET

P.M. GRIFFIN

ACE BOOKS, NEW YORK

FIRE PLANET

An Ace Book / published by arrangement with
the author

PRINTING HISTORY
Ace edition / November 1990

ISBN: 0-441-78334-1

Ace Books are published by The Berkley Publishing Group,
200 Madison Avenue, New York, New York 10016.
The name "ACE" and the "A" logo
are trademarks belonging to Charter Communications, Inc.

PRINTED IN THE UNITED STATES OF AMERICA

10 9 8 7 6 5 4 3 2 1

To my godson,
Dudley William Lamming, Jr.

ONE

"WELL DONE, BANDIT!" Varn Tarl Sogan called out to his winged comrade as she swerved into a sudden, seemingly impossibly sharp turn out of a full dive.

The gurry whistled to acknowledge his praise and came to him, nestling in the hand he raised and cupped to receive her.

The little feathered mammal was by far the strangest member of the elite Commando unit of which he was part, and to nearly everyone outside it, she seemed no more than a particularly endearing mascot—a seven-ounce ball of brown feathers with a thin stripe of black covering her bright, dark eyes like the mask of a pre-space Terran robber. A broad, supple, bright yellow bill gave further expression to her face, and equally vivid legs and feet served her as efficiently as any human's hands.

She was appealing, aye, but he and Islaen Connor, the woman who was both his commander and his consort, had not been long on Jade of Kuan Yin before they had come to realize that Bandit and her fellow gurries were something far more. They could converse thought-to-thought among themselves and with the individual humans with whom they bonded, and they could understand any language comprehensible to their humans. The Jadite creatures exerted a powerful influence upon most sentient life forms as well. By broadcasting enormous volumes of goodwill, they won for themselves and their companions the favor of all but the utterly depraved or those in the grip of overwhelming violent emotion.

Only his own team and Jade's settlers knew any of this, and

1

they held that knowledge in strictest secrecy, fearing what its revelation could mean for Jade and her small denizens.

He looked down at the gurry, now curled happily in his palm, and let her feel the full of his affection for her. He and his human comrades had long since given up trying to define what she was, but she reasoned and willed, and she had proven the depth of her love for them and her courage.

His eyes darkened until they appeared almost black. She had risked herself too often for their sake . . .

Bandit felt the cloud touch his mood and whistled in concern. *Varn?*

"Sorry, small one," he said, speaking aloud as he and Islaen usually did when alone with her despite her ability to take their response directly from their minds. "We are on furlough and should be putting the past behind us for now."

Yes!—Where's Islaen?

"Inside."

Sogan frowned. The Commando-Colonel had received a call from Admiral Sithe. If she was still tied up with that transmission, it probably meant trouble, yet he did not want to try contacting her lest he interrupt the conference . . .

He gave a mental shrug. If some new danger was looming before them, it was their business to meet and stop it, to see that the Federation's own vermin did not destroy from within what so many millions had fought and died to preserve during the decades of the great War. "We should go inside ourselves if you are finished out here," he told the gurry.

Bandit's finished!—Varn's pleased?

He smiled. "Aye, small one. You are a joy to watch."

The man gave a sigh of relief as he left the balcony and slid the doors closed behind them. Thorne of Brandine was the fairest world he had ever seen, and her air was like a song in one's throat, but she was cold for one accustomed to the Terra-standard temperatures normally maintained on most starships. Even with the cape he had thrown about his shoulders, the increasing evening chill had begun to bite at him.

The room in which he found himself was comfortably large with very fine, intricate engravings covering its walls and ceiling. The furnishings, too, were heavily carved but beautifully proportioned and fully functional, well befitting the palace'of a merchant prince, as this house had in fact been before Thorne's Doge had given it over to them for their headquarters and home.

Varn opened the top drawer of the desk standing beside the balcony's entrance and took from it a small metal box about half filled with dark brown flakes. "Here you go, Bandit, though that performance of yours merits a better reward than this."

The little hen gave an earsplitting whistle of pure delight. *Nothing's better!*

He laughed as she launched into his offering. Islaen had introduced Bandit to Terran milk chocolate early in their association, and it remained her favorite of all the sweets she had come to know and savor since.

His head raised, and he instinctively turned toward the main door. Even as they could share thoughts with their Jadite comrade, so, too, could his mind join with Islaen Connor's. That was an ability unique to them, and they guarded the secret of their strange talent and the gifts, different in each of them, that it gave them as closely as they did their knowledge of Bandit's intelligence and other powers. The life of a scientific curiosity had no appeal for either of them.

Commando-Colonel Islaen Connor came into the room a moment later. She was a comfortably tall, slender woman who moved with the grace of one well acquainted with the starlanes. Although she was still casually dressed, he saw, as he had half anticipated he would, that she had confined her rich auburn hair in the tightly pinned braid that was the nearly universal style adopted by female spacers. They had a mission, then, and would soon be lifting to take it up.

Islaen's finely wrought features had been grave when she entered, but she smiled in response to her husband's silent welcome, then shook her head in mock disapproval. *If you keep feeding her like that, she soon won't be able to rise off her perch.*

Nooo! the gurry protested. *Bandit's very careful!—Bandit deserves this! Varn said so!*

She does that. Sogan stroked the feathered head with the tip of his finger. *I think I can handle a starship or flier until I see her in action. Then I realize rather abruptly the difference between machine and reality.*

Bandit peered up at him anxiously. *Bandit's a gurry! Varn's human!*

"Meaning I am a dead ship in the air?" he challenged.

Nooo! Varn can do other things!

Varn!—"It's all right, love," the woman assured her. "He's just teasing you."

Her large, thickly lashed eyes fixed on the Commando-Captain, studying him intently.

He was moderately tall and well built, although he was wiry rather than heavily muscled, and he carried himself like one born to space and to the military. An air of command rested on him as if it were a cloak and the air of one long accustomed to bearing both peril and its consequences for himself and for others.

So he had, she thought. In the latter part of the War, Admiral Varn Tarl Sogan had led one of the finest and most successful of the Empire's fleets, and he remained an Arcturian war prince. The loss of military rank and the prerogatives of station in no way altered that.

Anger flashed momentarily in her eyes. That past, the role he had played and the place he had once occupied, could all too readily mean his death now. An officer's bearing was hardly uncommon in her war-torn ultrasystem, but Varn's hard, proud features and the hair and eyes that were the same dark brown color, a trait found only in the highest ruling families of the Empire's warrior caste, were plain for the reading, as several potentially bad incidents had already proven.

They had been lucky thus far, but the hatred engendered in the long War was powerful and often well founded, and the violence it could spark was not readily turned if it gained too much momentum. Even the awesome sacrifice Varn had made to spare Thorne of Brandine and his courage since then in defending threatened planets of his former enemies, which had brought him to the notice of her unit and won him his place with it, might not be sufficient to save him from a mob's or an assassin's wrath, even assuming he was given the time to relate that history.

She put that ever-present fear from her mind. It was something with which they had to live. Right now, it was his present condition she had to consider, the completeness of his recovery from the injuries he had sustained during their recent missions, not the scars, literal or figurative, left him by his people's executioners.

The former Admiral had felt this scrutiny from her often enough to read it accurately now. He faced her with a half smile as his mind opened to hers. *I am sound out, Colonel. This furlough has accomplished its purpose even if I would prefer that it had been allowed to continue to its proper end.*

You're a bit too sound-looking for this one if anything, she replied. *For once, you would have served us better by appearing a bit wan and off.*

His brows raised. *Just what does your Admiral Sithe have in mind for us?*

Islaen frowned slightly. He still could not accept in his heart that his place in the Federation, or maybe even with their own unit, was a real one . . .

There was no point in belaboring that. *Just some investigation work, or so we hope.*

Bandit flew to her shoulder. *We're leaving Thorne?* she asked in dismay.

"I'm afraid so, love. It is time—almost time, anyway—that we were getting back to work."

But Thorne's nice!

"You don't have to come with . . ." She winced as the hen's needle-sharp claws punctured the light Thornen fabric and the shoulder beneath. "Bandit, you scramble circuited little witch, power down! You should know by now that we wouldn't leave you behind, not unless you really wanted to stay."

Islaen and Varn need Bandit!

"Aye, we do. You've proven your value to us more than once."—*What are you laughing at, may I ask, Admiral? It seems to me that you didn't like the taste you got of her talons.*

One impaling was more than enough for me, he agreed, still laughing. *You did provoke it this time, however, so you are hardly entitled to much sympathy.*

Sogan grew serious again in the next moment. He drew the high-backed chair from beneath the desk for his commander and perched on the broad writing surface himself. *Where are we going, Islaen?*

Tambora of Pele.

He stared at her. *That is where Bethe and Jake are finishing off their honeymoon. What in space's name have they managed to dredge up now?*

Maybe nothing. They didn't like a few things they noticed, started hunting around, and got suspicious enough to contact Ram Sithe. He, in turn, did some more digging and called on us. She eyed him with some amusement. *We wound up fighting off a pirate armada on our honeymoon, if you recall. That's how you collected one of those stars decorating your dress uniform.*

I know, he responded gravely. *I have never made that up to you.*

Considering that we shared the accompanying credits, I really can't do much complaining, Islaen told him dryly.

The Federation rewarded its military and civilian citizens who performed with uncommon heroism in time of need practically as well as with the traditional symbols of honor. The citations they had won were all class one, and they had become a wealthy couple in their own right as a result.

His fingers brushed her marvelously pale cheek. *You deserved peace and delight, then, my Islaen. You still do.* His hand dropped to his side again. *What draws us to Tambora?*

Do you know anything about her?

The Arcturian shook his head. *Only that she has fine beaches and a good climate to lure Karmikel there,* he confessed. *I did not bother to read up on her.*

Neither did I until Ram Sithe faxmitted her file. I went through that before coming here.

The Commando-Colonel paused a moment to collect her thoughts, then went on. *She's an old world, originally colonized by people from Endor . . .*

He frowned. *They are mutants, are they not?*

Aye. There was no warmth in her reply. Despite all his basic sense of justice, despite the stark fact of his own mutation, proven by his powers of mind, Varn Tarl Sogan could not throw off his kind's revulsion for any race physically very different from the basic human prototype. It was one trait she strongly disliked in him, but at least it had never yet caused him to slight any of those he had encountered while serving with her unit, in person or in the duty he owed them. Of a certainty he had never desired, much less actively willed, the extermination of any such people, which was the chiefmost of all the Empire's crimes perpetrated upon both the worlds of their own ultrasystem and those they had conquered within the

Federation before the course of the War had at last turned, although neither had he probably questioned that policy until fate had thrown him among his former enemies and into enforced contact with all their many races and species. Thorne's offspring were as attractive to Arcturian as to Terran eyes . . .

Islaen shrugged that off. Whatever her feeling in the matter, one could not realistically expect a man to just cast off everything bred and trained into him from the moment of his conception. Besides, she had not acted out of pure, disinterested anger when she had gone up against the ancient enemies of her own race on their last mission. She had not overstepped stark need in the severity of the measures she had been compelled to adopt, and she had not permitted the slaughter to continue beyond the point where it could be stopped. She had taken no joy in the deaths of men—for that, she praised every god in the Federation—but the destruction of Britynon power at her hands and the breaking of their guilty government by the Navy fleet dispatched from Horus for that purpose, that had filled her with an exultation she now cringed to recall.

The war prince, for his part, kept tight shields over his own thoughts, closing his consort off from all but surface communication. *Their appearance is of no relevance,* he said stiffly with an apparent indifference that successfully concealed the instinctive disgust he felt. He knew that to be an illogical response, however powerless he was to quell it, and it was probably needless as well. They should have little enough to do with the on-worlders themselves, and Islaen Connor, as the unit's commander, would have to bear the brunt of that. He should be spared almost all of it. *What of Tambora herself? I should not have interrupted you.*

As I said, she's old. The colony was in place long before the Settlement Board was established, but her citizens have willed to take no part in the affairs of the Federation. They retained membership after achieving independence from colony status in order to hold the benefits that entails, but they refuse even to send representatives to the Senate, consenting to just accept the laws passed there provided they suffer no interference from the stars as a result.

Why should a people on that level of development so confine themselves? Sogan asked. *They were already Terra's seed-*

lings, not pre-spacers with the fear that their race's natural progress would be blighted by contact with a more advanced technology. And why have they refused the duties and privileges of your form of government? How do they dare refuse to assume their part in that?

Islaen shrugged. Tamborans consider any contact with other peoples as a temptation to depravity, as a kind of defilement in itself. Their first-ship settlers were members of a strict separatist sect, and they chose Tambora primarily because she suited their desire for total isolation so well. She's Terranormal, demanding no extraordinary aid or life support for human survival, and she's the only satellite circling Pele in a section of space poor in stars bearing planetary systems, none of which are anywhere near her. When the colony was founded, Tambora of Pele in truth lay at the very end of creation.

Friendly folk, he commented, not trying to conceal his growing disapproval.

Their clerics' policies proved so confining and economically disastrous that the colony very nearly smothered itself, but a vigorous civil leader took up the reins in time, and the Orange Ascetics faded into political oblivion after a couple of centuries.

Most of the populace now follow a gentler splinter group known as the Red Ascetics, but the original sect still exists in its old form and still exerts a strong moral influence on the entire population and the government, although its actual official membership is very small.

Varn's dark eyes narrowed. They had experienced problems enough on Anath of Algola, and it was only the chief leader there, the King, who had disliked off-world intervention. The rest of people had been behind their efforts.

Yet they do obviously have interstellar visitors, he observed. Witness our comrades.

The Noreenan nodded. Because Tambora is the only Federation world in a very large stretch of space, the Senate has always insisted on having a port at Strombolis, the capital, to serve as an emergency planeting site. This, the Tamborans have been forced to permit and to maintain, and they allow a small Patrol unit to be stationed there to police it, but that and *some unwanted but necessary exporting is the extent of the contact they allow between us.*

Their economic structure lets them get away with that. They have seen to it that they have very few actual requirements. The people are primarily agrarians, producing all they need and enough excess of a number of sugar crops for export to defray the expenses of the spaceport, including the paying and housing of the off-world specialists who must run it for them since no schooling in any such work is given to their own. Industry is extremely light and is strictly limited to the making of the few items each family group cannot fashion for itself.

Yet you say there are cities?

Aye. Strombolis houses about thirty thousand people. There are five other administrative communities with half that number, all connected by and servicing a planet-wide network of towns ranging in size from one hundred to two thousand adults, a number none are permitted to exceed, nor can any new towns or villages be established.

Stringent population control has always been necessary, she added. *There is little land to support them, no continents at all, just a vast number of islands, most of them small, scattered throughout one great planetary ocean. All of those appear to be the result of ancient volcanic activity.*

Varn shook his head in real puzzlement. *What moved Jake to suggest a hole like that for the final leg of his honeymoon, or for any leave, for that matter?*

Tambora of Pele is beautiful, and her climate's something out of a paradise. Off-worlders are unwelcome but not molested, and it's the resulting quiet that he wanted, the chance to completely bake out the last effects of our recent missions in total peace before having to go back to active duty again. In fact, the Navy used her now and then for that very purpose, particularly for those who had suffered repeated woundings or other trauma or who had existed long-term under severe stress. Commandos were those most frequently sent there either as individuals or in units after a series of missions or in the wake of penetration duty.

As for her citizens, it's too well known what the influx of alien ways from a powerful neighbor can do to a simpler society, pre-space or not. Their lifeway does limit them, but the same can be said in one sense or another about that of any other group. They consciously chose it, and its benefits have apparently continued to outweigh its faults for them. They're not really to be blamed for trying to protect it.

None of this indicates a pressing need for our attention, the former Admiral observed.

Tamborans are utterly pacific. They're not fools and appreciated full well the consequences of an Arcturian victory for a mutant people like themselves, and so they didn't protest sending their quota of recruits into the Navy. About the only stipulation they made was in refusing to allow any of their females to go off-world.

Her brows drew together in a frown. *Understand this, Varn. War and weapons are truly repugnant to them, to the point that they don't have so much as a police force or a watch of their own. They had a full noncombatant deferment, of course— there were plenty of medical and administrative duties to absorb them, freeing those willing to fight for service in the active fleets—but even so, those returning home were still required to enter the official Red Ascetic monasteries for extensive purification and probably retraining before being allowed to go back to their residences and former activities.*

Despite all this, despite the aversion with which even nonviolent off-world work was viewed, a certain number of them, nearly twenty percent of the recruits by the War's end, refused to accept their deferment. They claimed that it was black hypocrisy to take it since they would only be allowing the Navy to use some other soldiers for its slaughter work.

Varn Tarl Sogan straightened. *What?* Everything Islaen had said before sounded logical for these people whom he was beginning to detest. This was something different.

There's more yet, the Commando-Colonel added significantly. *Go on.*

That was the line proposed by the Gray Ascetics, as the old sect has called itself since throwing off their bright robes in mourning over their people's decision to remain part of the Federation at the time of their gaining full planetary status. They also gave no opposition when those acting upon it were banished to a colony site on Albion's moon, which Tambora leased for that purpose.

Within the last couple of years, however, they have declared that a great injustice had been done to those men, and their Abbot has arranged to have a large number of them pardoned and repatriated as part of his community.

Sogan's breath hissed between his teeth. *I like none of this, Islaen. Perhaps these clerics are indeed trying to do a commendable thing and salvage those who seemed irrevocably lost. It would be understandable if they are also trying to seize the opportunity to regain something of their old status numerically and through the inevitable gratitude of the exiles' family groups. However, it is possible as well that they may have something more sinister in mind.*

The formation of a ready-made army already trained to act decisively and physically if need be?

Aye.

She nodded. *That's precisely what Jake and Bethe thought. The present government has no ability to defend itself against any such attack, and the populace is conditioned to accept the commands of those in authority, which the Gray Robes have always enjoyed in large measure.*

Nasty, he commented, *but what are we supposed to do about it, even if it proves true? This appears to be a strictly surplanetary affair, and according to your Federation's law, the Navy has no right to interfere.*

As it stands, we have no power whatsoever to act, except of course, to make sure nothing interferes with the running of the spaceport. If the Gray Robes take over, you can put credits down that they'll try to close that fast. They've never ceased opposing and condemning everything connected with it.

Her eyes suddenly pierced his. *We have not only the right but the stark duty to prevent a massacre of off-world personnel.*

A massacre? From that bunch of . . .

She nodded. *The psychomedics believe it could happen, although it's probable that the Gray Abbot himself hasn't even considered the possibility.*

Her hands swept out in a somewhat helpless gesture. *His followers are now at a high pitch of gratitude-fired fanaticism piled upon their horror of what they've done and witnessed and fury against those they hold to be responsible. Turn the lot of them loose in a pack, release some of the psychological holds keeping all that raw emotion in check, and nearly anything could happen, most of it very bad.*

Have they held onto their arms?

That was a critical question. Because they were essential to survival itself throughout most of the war-ravaged ultrasystem, the Navy permitted its personnel to retain their hand blasters upon demobilization. Pacifists, though, would logically dispose of all such gear as soon as they legally could.

She shook her head. *No, not most of them. That was one of the first things Admiral Sithe had checked out. Some few may have hung onto their weapons for one reason or another, but nearly all the Tamborans did, in fact, either return or sell their blasters.*

Their would-be leaders would be expecting nothing else from them. Those men are poor raw material for bringing about a coup. No pretraining or plotting was possible with them. They simply had to suffer the shock of exposure to battle and then be allowed to taste the despair of exile for a while before anyone could hope to bring them to a state in which they would be amenable to taking part in any such extreme act. The Gray Robe Abbot can't be counting on any superabundance of arms coming in with his troops.

The Arcturian shook his head. *It does not compute, Islaen. A handful of blasters might be sufficient to pull down a totally unarmed surplanetary government such as you describe, but the spaceport is another matter.*

Don't be so sure. A large mob acting with speed and without any forewarning is a deadly force. The like have swept away heavily armed garrisons throughout Terran history.

The man was silent for several minutes. *That is an outside possibility,* he said at last. *I do not believe Sithe would send us in for that, not with Bethe and Karmikel already on-world. You must have more.*

We do, she replied grimly. *Two weeks ago, a shipment of mixed armaments disappeared from one of the Navy warehouses on Alpha Gary. There might be no connection and probably isn't, but Commandos who put too much trust in coincidence don't tend to live very long.* She smiled coldly. *At least, it gives us grounds to begin an investigation. Stolen Navy weapons are our business, and so is their transport or sale or any harm to civilian or service populations that might arise from their use.*

Islaen Connor flexed her shoulders as if in sudden weariness. *We'll have to be careful all the same. This situation's delicate. The Navy can't ride on all burners over Federation planets, and we'll be disowned and slapped down fast if we're caught overstepping ourselves, particularly if we happen to be wrong about any part of this.*

We shall need some excuse for going there. No newly united couple would just summon their commanding officers to their side.

They would this time. It seems Tamborans don't like inoculations very much, either, and require that their citizens take only those demanded by Federation law. As a result, a number of usually minor infections are endemic there. Normally, they see only a few cases of each in a given year, but our comrades arrived at the tail end of a major outbreak of Ambrosian Flu. There isn't nearly enough antibonding serum to go around on-world, and the Patrol was called upon for a rescue. Jake found out from their Sergeant and promptly volunteered us.

A medical run is Stellar Patrol work, is it not?

It's anyone's work who's capable of doing it best. This is the real thing, friend, not some conveniently manufactured supposed emergency. —There aren't many starships that can outfly the Fairest Maid, *and Ram Sithe has already dispatched the serum. We'll rendezvous with the fighter carrying it en route.*

The war prince accepted the rebuke. In the Empire, too, a call for medical aid received this same attention and priority, and the situation before them merited it. Ambrosian Flu was nothing in itself, no more than a mild respiratory infection, but in a few rare cases, the virus could mutate, migrate to the reproductive cells, egg or sperm, and settle there, breaking certain genes in the process. The result for the offspring of any such carrier was tragic. One simple injection prevented that, destroyed the altered organisms entirely, but the serum remained effective for only a limited time after its production, and it required a fast ride if it was to fulfill its purpose across the vast reaches of interstellar space.

The Tamborans will accept this kind of help?

They're not complete vacuum brains. It's to retain access to such services that they stayed with the Federation in the first place. Her mouth tightened. *Even the Gray Robes apparently can't bring themselves to allow babies to be born without arms. At least, they haven't made any protest.*

Islaen forced herself back to their own business. *That run plus my rank will almost certainly gain us at least one audience with the Commissar, the surplanetary leader. If we're lucky, I may be able to pick up something useful then.*

Maybe, her husband cautioned. *None of the conspirators may be present.*

If he's severely threatened enough to be transmitting fear or deep concern, I'll know it. That would give us an indication that we were navigating on the right charts, at least, and perhaps hint at our time frame as well.

Islaen Connor could not read thoughts except with Sogan or Bandit, but she did have the ability to receive the emotions of human-level individuals, even as her consort could pick up those of most animals. It was a talent that had served her unit well during the War and in the almost equally deadly time since its ending.

Varn had seen proof in plenty of its usefulness, but now he shook his head. No gift, however strong, would help them if they were not given the opportunity to exercise it. *He could just thank us and wish us a speedy voyage home,* he warned.

She smiled. *We were both injured on our last jaunt, remember? We may be rather too well recovered to win much sympathy, but that's been the case with many of those the Navy sent for final R&R on Tambora. It shall be my decision to take advantage of her peace and climate to be sure that we are fully ready to assume our duties when the time to do so comes. It'll also make ready sense that we'd want to lift as a unit instead of having to waste time meeting up with Jake and Bethe somewhere in the starlanes later on.*

Will we be given the freedom to work?

Oh, aye. There're some restrictions, right enough, but the island as a whole's open to off-worlders.

The gurry had listened patiently to the humans' discussion. Now she fluttered to the back of Islaen's flight chair. *Bandit can help, too?*

"Almost certainly, love. I'm not sure what'll be needed from any of us, but you've never yet failed to aid our cause, particularly in difficult diplomatic situations. You'll be an asset to the party."

She stroked the hen thoughtfully. "The Spirit of Space willing, a few unpleasant encounters with the locals'll be all we have to face on this one." She glanced at Varn although she continued speaking aloud. "This is supposed to be just an investigation, not a battle assignment. With any luck at all, it might actually end up that way."

TWO

THE VOYAGE TO Tambora of Pele was quiet, unbroken by any alarm, and had time been pressing them less strenuously, all three, humans and gurry, would have enjoyed it thoroughly. There was a particular peace and grandeur in interstellar space for those who knew it and respected the challenges it represented, a serenity that was not to be found in any other environment, and it drew them powerfully, secure as they were in their confidence in their ship and in themselves.

At last, however, the *Fairest Maid* entered Pele's system and drew perceptibly nearer to her sole satellite until Tambora filled most of the near-space viewer.

Her beauty left them breathless. The planet was exquisite, very like Terra in appearance at this distance, but the blue showing beneath the thick, white marbling of clouds was not the true, cool shade of the Federation's mother world. It was, rather, the exotic, brilliant turquoise of the sun-warmed tropical seas comprising the vastly greater part of her surface.

I hope our comrades are wrong, Islaen Connor, Varn Tarl Sogan said softly. *She is too fair to suffer the kind of evil our kind too often spawns.*

Too fair indeed, Islaen replied, screening her sadness from him lest it deepen the weight she could feel pressing on him.

They fell silent again and watched as the lovely planet loomed ever larger in the *Maid*'s screens. It would not be much longer now before they had to strap down in preparation for planeting.

Suddenly the Commando-Colonel realized that Sogan was

scowling darkly and had been for some minutes. She glanced sharply at him. *What's wrong, Varn?*

I have been thinking about those tapes we studied. About the information they did not contain. His eyes narrowed. *There is too much mystery about this Tambora for a planet that has been settled so long. It is incomprehensible why a world whose entire land surface is of volcanic origin has never had so much as a basic seismic profile done.*

He did not try to conceal his concern. The homeworlds of his ultrasystem were geophysically dead, utterly quiet, and when their armadas had invaded the very different planets comprising the Federation, Arcturian war leaders had failed to take into consideration the potential for disaster seething in various surplanetary phenomena. It was one lesson Ruling Command had never seemed able to learn, and right until the War's end, they had continued to post men on unstudied or poorly studied planets. Countless soldiers of the Empire had perished needlessly as a result, shattered by savage, mindless forces to which they should never have been exposed. To his mind, that was no less than a betrayal, stark criminal negligence bordering upon treason itself.

She was colonized long before the Settlement Board was established as I told you, Islaen replied, *and not only haven't her people asked for any studies, they've absolutely denied the requests of several groups who have wished to conduct them over the centuries.*

So your information indicates. I would like to know why.

The Noreenan woman recognized what lay behind the sharpness in his tone. Sogan had suffered as an officer and personally because of his Ruling Command's laxity with respect to Mirelle of Eri, and he knew too well what had happened elsewhere. He could not be blamed for not wanting to find himself in the power of any such blind force now.

Tamborans don't like having off-worlders wandering around. They have little use for most minerals and the like themselves and don't want to take the chance of something being discovered that might act as a lure to strangers.

That is arrant neglect of public safety! How can Federation authorities permit . . .

Islaen Connor sighed. *The Senate can't just send in a fleet to sweep down and violate the will of a member planet. Millions of us died to prevent your lot from doing that to us. Like it or not, this is Tambora's own business, and we'll just have to leave it at that.*

There is nothing that can be done in a situation like this? he persisted.

The Colonel shook her head. *Not a bloody thing, friend. If there were a death-peril emergency, aye, then the Navy or even the Stellar Patrol might temporarily seize command under certain circumstances, particularly if off-worlders were threatened as well, but woe to the officer who overreacted and exercised that option without real cause.*

Potential volcanic upheaval should supply that.

Tambora's volcanoes are extinct. Never once in all the centuries since the first explorers planeted has there been the least bit of trouble from that source anywhere on her surface.

Maybe you are right, the war prince conceded wearily after a brief pause.

He gave her a wan smile. *I seem to be seeking out trouble, and needlessly. Our own work is likely to give us more than enough of that.*

Enough to keep all five of us well occupied, Admiral.

The Arcturian forgot all his gloomy concerns once the *Fairest Maid* was down and he and his companions stepped out onto the boarding ramp for their first breath of Tamboran air.

The spaceport was a small one and occupied a site a little apart and to the left of the capital, right at the edge of the nearly tideless ocean. It was so situated as to give a fine view of the city and the high country behind it.

Strombolis was a crescent-shaped, tightly clustered community set on a series of low hills just beyond the broad beach area with its dark gray sand and gently lapping turquoise waters.

The whole island, the planet's largest by a great margin, was the top of an immeasurably huge mountain, and the shore fell away rapidly, allowing boats of considerable size to dock fairly close to the beach.

The city itself was a pretty one. Most of the dwellings were small, but they were nicely constructed and were painted a restful pale green. Only the larger public buildings were white or, more rarely, yellow. The streets were narrow, purposely so to discourage vehicular traffic, and followed the flow of the land rather than any rigid grid.

Behind Strombolis, towering over the entire scene, stood the Dragon.

It was a mountain out of an artist's vision, tall, conical in form, cloaked in vivid green right to its highest point. The luxuriant growth spilled over without break into the ancient crater that plainly revealed the peak's history and had motivated the first settlers to christen it as they had. The upper portion of that inner wall was visible from the city and the spaceport through a deep, V-shaped notch in the otherwise high walls surrounding it.

Seventeen fast little streams had their birth on the Dragon's slopes, one of which ran right through the heart of the city. Water from the frequent rains kept them filled and added force to their currents so that all had carved deep channels for themselves, slicing through the fertile soil into the volcanic bedrock below.

Varn drew a deep, satisfied breath, glad to be free of the processed gas supporting life aboard the starship. Tambora was fair even beyond the promise of her near-space beauty . . .

His nose wrinkled as he caught a faint, fleeting scent, sulfur or something akin to it, and he glanced in annoyance at the vessel berthed nearest them, one of a half-dozen others currently on-world.

She was no beauty, an elderly freighter whose skin was dark from long, hard service with little overhauling and pockmarked with dents left by meteors and the Spirit of Space only knew what else.

Her crew were manhandling canisters out of her hold, and he sighed to himself, momentarily sympathizing with the Tamborans' desire to keep strangers and their chemicals away from this paradise they had made their own.

The taint vanished from the air almost as he became aware of it, and he had forgotten it entirely by the time he spotted a small group of people approaching the *Fairest Maid* a few minutes later.

There were six, all clad in the uniform of the Stellar Patrol and walking, although not marching, in formation.

They were a mixed bunch, as was usual with a Patrol company. The noncom at their head and one of the Yeomen

were typical Sirenians, tall and slim with aristocratic features
and eyes and hair black enough to stand well against their
russet complexions. There was but one mutant, a woman
whose feather-like hair and distinctly feathered hands proclaimed her to be a daughter of Avis. The other woman and the
two remaining men were strongly built and of a basically
Terran appearance. They could have originated on any one of
nearly countless planets settled by people whose line had come
into being on the mother world.

Islaen gave a regretful glance at the glistening, crescent-
shaped starship berthed to their right. Jake Karmikel and Bethe
Danlo were aboard their *Jovian Moon* and had already given
their comrades welcome via transceiver, but they would wait
until the serum had been transferred to the Patrol unit before
coming aboard themselves. None of them undervalued the
most immediate reason for the *Maid*'s presence here, and until
that mission had been completed, both other work and pleasure
would have to remain on hold.

The ebony-haired Sergeant stopped and saluted smartly
when she came within easy speaking distance of the pair.
"Sergeant Abana Janst reporting with the Tamboran Patrol
unit, Colonel Connor."

The Commando-Colonel returned her salute and, after
introducing her companion, told the company to board.

Abana paused to stroke Bandit, who had perched on the rail
of the ramp and whistled self-importantly for attention.

The Patrol agent's beautiful, serious face softened into a
smile. "She's wonderful, Colonel. Your friends didn't exag-
gerate at all in describing her."

Islaen's eyes sparkled. The gurry was starting off well with
her usual job of creating good public relations for the team.
"She's a delight, right enough."

Yes!

The Noreenan laughed softly in thought. *I know, little minx!
Let's just hope your magic works equally well on the locals
when we have to deal with them.*

Bandit will try, Islaen.

I know that, too, love, she replied seriously.

By this time, the Patrol agents had reached the entrance
lock.

"You'll probably want to check out the serum as soon as possible," she remarked to Abana.

"Aye, and distribute it as fast as we can. They've been inoculating only the highest risk cases, but even so, they've completely run out. The port aid station donated its stock this morning, but that won't be the equal of a drop in all that ocean out there. It's probably gone even now."

"Replace that before turning the shipment over," Islaen Connor advised. "You might find it a bit hard to pry a payback out of them later, or to get the Patrol to replenish your store once the emergency's over, for that matter."

"There's enough?"

"More than enough," she assured her. "This business got prime treatment all down the line."

"Nice thinking, Colonel. We'll pull out our share before contacting the Commissar." The Sirenian woman smiled. "Rest assured that you're both—all three of you," she corrected herself, "welcome on Tambora, by the port staff, at least. The planet herself may be a jewel, but our hosts' attitude makes her a regular hole. Visitors from the stars are usually seen as a proper treat." The black eyes sparkled. "Especially illustrious visitors."

"Jake's taken it on himself to recount some of our history, I take it?" she asked dryly.

"No need. Your name and Captain Sogan's are as well known in our service as they probably are to the Navy rank and file, at least out here on the rim."

Abana's voice grew more serious. "I confess that all of us feel a lot easier having you here after the near miracles you've pulled off in the past."

The Commando sighed. "Miracles don't always work. —Every mission's different. We're just supposed to be fact-finding on Tambora, and I hope we discover we're dead wrong in our fears. In any event, we probably won't be called upon to do anything, whatever we learn, except to pass the intelligence on to the appropriate people."

"Well, no matter what you dredge up and decide to do with it, the Patrol's behind you. We'll take your orders without quibbling about differences in our respective services."

Islaen eyed the Patrol-Sergeant somberly. "We could need that help. Thanks."

She glanced toward the core ladder, which gave access to the various levels of the starship. "Could you come back up to the crew's cabin once you've finished examining the serum? Varnt and I would like to hear your appraisal of the situation here as soon as possible."

Varnt Sogan was the halfalias the desperately injured war prince had accidentally given himself when his rescuers had misunderstood his slurred response to their questions after they had pulled him out of space; his supposedly dead body had been set adrift in an aged lifecraft following his execution. Because of the brutality with which he had been used, those caring for him had assumed he was yet another victim of the Arcturians, not an officer—former officer—of the Empire's once-invincible Navy.

That barely altered version of his own name would be no defense against anyone even vaguely suspecting his origins, but when Sogan had seen what had happened, he realized he might encounter even worse difficulties if he attempted to change his story. He had determined to live and live free as best he might, both in compliance with the apparent will of his ultrasystem's cruel gods and in a kind of defiance of them, instead of putting a blaster to his head, as would more logically be expected of one of his caste and station in these inconceivable circumstances. Any tampering with the newly born identity fate had given him could too readily have shattered it, dooming him to death, imprisonment, or, worst of all, a return to his own people and either a second savage execution or perpetual disgrace.

Abana Janst nodded her assent at once. "Of course. My crew can unload the serum and arrange to have it transferred to the Tamborans. I have to make the actual delivery myself, of course, but you should be finished with me long before we're ready for that."

"Good. —The *Maid*'s Varnt's baby. He'll show you to the hold and answer any questions that come up. In the meantime, I'll be getting our notes together."

THREE

ABANA STOPPED AT the door of the small but comfortable crew's cabin, that in which the starship's staff and rare passengers spent their off-duty waking hours, and gave salute. "The serum checks out fine, Colonel. It'll be in Tamboran hands within twenty minutes after we get the last of it out of your hold."

"Excellent. It will be a relief to have it where it's needed. —Sit down," Islaen instructed, pointing to a table surrounded on three sides by padded benches that occupied one end of the cabin. "I've programmed the range. I figured you could probably use a hot cup of jakek as much as I do."

"It'll go down right," the other woman agreed.

Varn nodded his thanks and slid into his customary place after taking one of the cups she was holding. He smiled at her but said nothing in voice or in mind. Bandit, too, kept still as she perched on the edge of the table.

Abana sipped the dark, steaming liquid, then raised a brow appreciatively. The jakek might not be of the quality found in the finer restaurants of Hedon or Siren, but it was damn good. "If this is a sample of the *Maid*'s fare, I'll ship out on her anytime."

"We do our best to keep life reasonably bearable." The Commando-Colonel sat beside her husband. "You know why we're here, apart from the medical run?"

"The possible coup? Aye." Her mouth hardened. "We should all be cashiered for not spotting that ourselves."

"Jake just came on the scene with a fresh outlook, that's all. It's happened like that countless times in the past.—You've been stationed on Tambora some time?"

The Sirenian nodded. "Two years. We relieved the last company after their three-year tour was up. No one stays longer than that."

"You know that port and its visitors fairly well?" Sogan asked her.

"Aye, of course. We have little other scope for activity, and so we've concentrated rather heavily on what goes on here."

"That will prove valuable to us now." Islaen detailed the threat posed by the Alpha Gary theft and the real risk the port personnel faced in the event a rebellion, armed or not, went out of control.

Sergeant Janst listened gravely, but when the Noreenan had finished, she shook her head. "I can't speak for the future, but I can say pretty certainly that nothing like that's come in as of now. In fact, apart from the serum you've brought, there haven't been any shipments to the locals at all. Tamborans don't import. They don't want anything off-worlders offer. All inbound cargo is for the spaceport itself and is handled by the port's own staff."

"All of it?" Sogan interjected, frowning slightly. "You are positive of that?"

She smiled at his doubt. "This isn't Horus, Captain. Not much traffic comes here, and we know the most of it well."

"What about planetings elsewhere? This is not Tambora's only island."

The Sirenian shook her head. "Possible in theory, but not likely. The other islands are nearly all very small, and to a one, they're too mountainous to make even acceptable planeting sites. A starship's master would have to be very desperate or very well paid indeed to attempt setting down on even the best of them. Besides, they're all populated. A ship couldn't just sneak in."

"Not unless the inhabitants suffered from selective blindness," the Colonel pointed out.

"These people aren't much for intrigue, and those living off the main island are even more sensitive about interacting with off-worlders than Strombolis' citizens are."

"What about the Gray Robes? They'd do what their Abbot wanted, wouldn't they, especially the former exiles?"

"That's our one worry, but to our knowledge, they have no off-island monasteries." She shook her head. "A couple of men could be sent anywhere to take the shipment, aye, but they'd still need local help to conceal it and local silence, and I just can't see any Tamboran community consenting to that. Weapons are weapons to their minds. They wouldn't have to fire them themselves to hold themselves responsible for bloodshed caused by any arms they helped import."

Islaen sighed. "You haven't given us much to go on. No likely planetings elsewhere, and you claim the official traffic is clean."

She nodded. "I'd lay a year's pay on that. The ships using the port are regulars. They're scarcely the glory of the ultrasystem, and their crews wouldn't find themselves at home in the salons of Siren, but they're straight enough for their kind."

"You know that for a fact, not merely believe it?"

Abana inclined her head in assent. "Aye. They're an unruly lot as a whole, and we've had our troubles with them—minor fights, intoxication of various types, things of that nature. I was concerned enough about some of them in the beginning of our tour that I had finger and voice prints run on them. It seemed like a good idea, so I've continued doing it with all those setting down here and with those working in the port as well. I can more or less vouch for all the off-worlders on Tambora."

"Why check the port hands?" Varn inquired curiously.

"Many of them find little to do here apart from their work, and I was afraid of contraband intoxicants coming in. There is also good reason to fear personality problems."

She eyed him. "If you feel I've overreached myself, I guess you'll have to take that up with my superiors, but I'm in command here and have acted as I thought advisable."

"That's not our concern, Sergeant," Islaen Connor interjected quickly. "Right now, the knowledge you've gained is to our benefit and to Tambora's.—What about the ships' activities when they're not in port?"

"Nothing very dramatic. None of them are capable of doing much in the way of raiding, and even if they were, these are planet-hoppers. They earn their way, such as it is, by making short runs at frequent intervals. They can account for their time and have their claims corroborated by one planet or another during every one of the few incidents Prince Sector's had."

"What about strangers?"

"Few come, no more than a half dozen since I've been on-world, all of whom have checked out. There's nothing to draw anyone to Tambora apart from rare emergencies. The rim isn't pushing out at this point, so we don't get the explorers or settlers, and trade throughout all the Sector's both light and of poor quality."

"It all sounds very reasonable, but your security measures belie your assurances," Varn Tarl Sogan told her.

"As I've mentioned, these spacers are rough. Take your neighbor over there, the one that was servicing her holds when we came aboard. Her crew can be real nasty if crossed, but the *Rounder*'s clean for all that. She's had to work plenty hard for precious little gain, and it's left its mark on those manning her. That's the way it is with most of the rest of them, too."

Abana sighed. "If we've concentrated a lot of effort on this, you can put that down to boredom on our part as much as anything else. Breaking up portside brawls is the work of a surplanetary police force, not the Stellar Patrol, but that's what we're reduced to doing here since the Tamborans won't demean themselves by taking care of it."

She leaned forward suddenly. "I'm not whining. This is an assignment, and we could've drawn a lot worse, but I'll tell you this much. If word gets out that a revolution's brewing and that things might get bad on Tambora, every man and woman in the port would promptly pack up, get off-world on all burners, and let the locals have the full joy of their new overlords."

"Your unit along with the rest?" he asked coldly.

"We're Patrol!" she snapped. "We'd stay, and we'd fight, for all the good it would do against a really wild mob, whether it was armed with those Navy weapons or not. Even if we did manage to survive, it wouldn't make much difference to the outcome for the present government or to the fate of the planet long-term, and by the Spirit of Space, there's plenty in me to gloat over that fact."

"Why?" Islaen Connor asked. "Why this bitterness, Sergeant? No one dealing with Tamborans has described them as likable, but neither has any complaint been lodged against them according to the records I've seen."

"Those compiling them very obviously never spent any

appreciable time on Tambora of Pele! —No, they are not malignant people or intentionally cruel. Their lifeway's clean. They abhor violence. They're scrupulously honest in all their dealings. I'll give them that and a great deal more besides.

"However, Siren's towers spiraled high and fair long before Terra's offspring ever thought to penetrate even her own near-space, yet all those centuries of civilization have not served to weaken us in spirit or heart, in mind or body.

"Baalbeer's forebears were among the first to leave your mother world for the stars and dared to make Avis their own although nothing human should have been able to survive in her trees, much less flourish there.

"Each of the others in my unit is the product and continuation of a history of courage and striving, and all of us rightly feel proud of the planets and the civilizations that formed us.

"The same is true of each of the port workers. It's true of those utilizing it. Those spacers have a multigrav struggle just to survive, and neither they nor any of the rest of us enjoy being targets for contempt merely because we didn't happen to arise from a small band who left Endor long ago because they couldn't get on with their neighbors."

Her eyes flashed. "It's easy to be tolerant of their ways when you have to spend only a few days here once in the course of your life, but it's something different to live where you're regarded as a source of contamination, one best avoided if at all possible, as would be the plague center of a particularly loathsome disease.

"That we look different from Tambora's offspring is unforgivable, that we live and choose to live in a manner somewhat unlike theirs is obscene, that we dare think along other lines is most diabolical of all, and though these Tamborans condemn each of our races and lifeways with admirable impartiality, they still despise us all as traitors for having left our own planets and societies and willingly mingled with people other than our own.

"They want to hold themselves aloof from any possible lure our ways or goods might have and so try to avoid interaction with us save when need demands, as at the sale of a crop, for instance, and then some of them act as though they were defiled merely by breathing the same air as a space hound. I've witnessed a few of those transactions, and you can believe that I'm not exaggerating."

Varn cringed in his own mind. The Tamborans were not the only fitting targets for that tirade . . .

His voice did not betray his disquiet. "They would be disciples of the Gray Ascetics, I suppose?"

Abana looked at him sharply. "Aye.—You used your travel time well."

"Not well enough to have recognized there was a full-blown morale problem here," he replied quietly. "It could well affect our mission, yet we were given no indication that it existed."

"Someone damn well should realize it! Hasn't it struck anyone back in brass hat paradise as a little bit strange that not a single person has ever signed up for a second tour on a planet with a climate like Tambora's, that no one will call for his family, and that those who had originally made arrangements before their arrival here to have their kin transported to join them after they were settled have invariably canceled those requests within their first month on-world?"

She paused and forced some of the sharpness from her voice. "I said before that I'm not whining, and I meant it. The Patrol is better off than most of the other off-worlders. Our skills aren't being rightly utilized, and we do chafe at that, but we know that our chief work here is to serve as a check against trouble.

"At that, we succeed. Our number may be small, but it would still be a foolish wolf pack that would choose to draw too close attention from our cruiser, and so the lanes in this area have remained fairly free of their activities. There have been no clashes between port people and the Tamborans despite what has, mistakenly or otherwise, been taken for provocation, because it is appreciated that we'll act fast and hard if someone starts anything, whatever our sympathies might be. The unit we relieved handled two space rescues, the participants in both earning class-two heroism citations as a result. —We know we're serving good purpose on Tambora of Pele, and so we give that service willingly."

Her eyes met and held his although there was that in the Commando-Captain that made such contact disturbing. "I wouldn't have said anything or let myself go like this, but if there is to be trouble, I thought it best that you know the full

situation." She shook her head. "I wouldn't want to put any
credits down on how much help you can count on from the
port, or what kind, apart from what my unit'll give."

"I'm glad you did speak," Islaen told her grimly. "We do
have some influence, or our commander does. We'll try to
arrange to have the tour time on Tambora halved or, better still,
brought down to one year."

"That'll be expensive!" the Sirenian exclaimed.

"Not as expensive as ruining skilled people and maybe
seeing something really nasty explode here. There's certainly
potential enough for that."

The Sergeant gave her a wry smile. "I'm truly sorry,
Colonel. You two came to Tambora with one problem, and
now I've put another on top of it."

"On the contrary," Varn assured her. "You have just about
removed the greatest of our concerns. We must still confirm
that your assessment is accurate, of course, but I doubt now
that we shall have to contend with heavy off-world weapons,
whatever does take place here.

"As for the rest, if the Stellar Patrol is like the Navy, you
should be in line for a commendation for your handling of the
conditions you found here."

There had been no apparent change in him, no alteration in
look or voice, but Abana Janst felt pride rise within her at his
words, and she realized for the first time that this man was no
mere possessor of rank but a leader, a commander, in the full
sense of the word, one of those whose like had made both the
Navy and the Stellar patrol all that they had proven themselves
to be.

She remained sunk in thought for several minutes. The
Commandos might be somewhat reassured after her report, but
there were too many gaps in her knowledge for them to accept
her conclusions as final. Ferreting out and confirming the
actual facts was not likely to be a simple chore. "The Commissar will see you both tomorrow to thank you for the speedy
delivery of that serum—I was asked to deliver the invitation
when I reported you were preparing to planet—but after that,
you'll be on the same footing as the rest of us. In fact, he'll be
more eager than usual to be rid of you, your profession being
what it is. What excuse will you make for staying?"

"The same one the Navy used during the War. We were both

hit in the course of our last mission, and I'll tell him I want to take advantage of Tambora's quiet and climate for a good rest before our next assignment."

"You're a healthy-looking pair of former invalids," the agent observed.

"All the same, our story can readily be checked should the Commissar choose to make the inquiry."

"You're still very obviously well now, and any furlough you take here will be seen as being by your own choosing. Can you carry it off with so little scope for normal pleasure activities?"

Varn Tarl Sogan gave her the ghost of a smile. "It is fairly apparent that I am a loner, and Islaen has booked passage with me. We would naturally spend some time with our comrades and perhaps a little with your unit. Beyond that, no one should see it as odd that we should prefer to spend our time familiarizing ourselves with the port and its people and exploring and enjoying Tambora herself rather than seeking out more hectic pastimes. It should not even be suspected that we are seeking anything in particular if we are at all circumspect."

He frowned slightly. "Islaen tells me we will have no trouble gaining access to the rest of the island."

"No. Our hosts don't formally object to our traveling on-world provided we cause no damage. We can even remain outside the port area for several days as long as we camp in a different place each evening and keep away from Tamboran buildings. Similarly, we're permitted free access to Strombolis, though we may not pass the night there, of course."

She paused. "As a matter of fact," she said thoughtfully, "it wouldn't be a bad idea for your comrades or one of us to give you a quick tour around the city later today so you can get the general lay of the place."

She came to her feet. "I'd best be checking on my crew now. There really is a big need to get that serum into the Tamboran hospitals as quickly as possible."

"Thanks for the rundown," the Commando-Colonel told her. "It'll shorten our search and help keep us navigating in the right lanes for the rest."

"Glad to do what I can, Colonel Connor. —Give a call if you need us. In the meantime, we'll keep our eyes open and let you know if we pick up anything."

* * *

No sooner had the Patrol transport pulled away from the *Fairest Maid* than Jake's voice sounded over the transceiver requesting permission to board. Minutes later, he exploded into the crew's cabin and caught his commander up in an exuberant bear hug.

Commando-Captain Jake Karmikel was a bigger man than his Arcturian comrade, taller and considerably broader of shoulder, though he was by no means muscle-bound. He was good-looking, with Noreen's fair skin and the red hair with which she often gifted her offspring. His eyes were a bright, clear blue.

His companion was a contrast to him, at least with respect to size. Bethe Danlo was a very small woman and slight even for her height. Her features were pleasant and proclaimed a Terran origin although her line had been space-bred since the days before the formal founding of the Federation. Her hair was a fine golden blond and was confined in the ubiquitous coronet, even as Islaen's was. The eyes were slate blue, steady and assured, bespeaking the willingness and ability to face the challenges fate sent.

She slid into the seat opposite Varn and scooped the waiting gurry into her hands. "How's my little pet these days?" she asked as she planted a kiss on the upturned head. "Are these two feeding you right, or are they starving you in some silly attempt to watch your weight, which you're well able to do yourself?"

Bandit answered with a shrill whistle since only Sogan and Islaen were able to receive her thoughts.

Bethe glanced at the Arcturian. "I take it that means, aye, she's fine, Admiral?"

"It does. That feathered rogue sees to it that she gets what she wants." His eyes went to the other two, and he laughed. "Do you approve of such behavior in your husband, Sergeant?"

"Oh, aye. It saves my ribs for a while. —Just be glad he doesn't accost you in a similar manner."

"I am," he replied, wishing at the same time that he could bring himself to do as much with Islaen even when they were alone.

The gurry returned to him momentarily. *Bethe's nice!* she enthused.

Aye, small one. She is that.

He had liked the demolitions expert from their first meeting on Hades of Persephone and felt comfortable with her.

He liked Karmikel as well, but he was conscious of how poorly he still stood up against the long-term Commando in most of their on-world work, and he had not forgotten the close relationship Jake had shared with Islaen Connor. They had entered Basic training at the same time and had served together until the War's end and after.

Varn lived in the fear that the Noreenan woman would someday regret the choice she had made between them. She would not betray the vows she had taken, but to have her bound to him in error, recognizing her error . . .

His fingers brushed the grip of his blaster. That, he would not permit. His death would in itself be a cruel blow for her, but better that than an ever-constricting chain.

Bandit looked up at him inquisitively, and he quickly pulled his thoughts back to his surroundings. He tested his mind shields and found them tight enough that his consort should not have picked up his short-lived gloom in the excitement of the moment. He hoped by all the Federation's gods that she had not; she would not be pleased to know that he still harbored something of this doubt.

Islaen at last wriggled free of her old comrade's embrace and took her place beside Sogan. "Sit down, you space tramp, and say hello to Bandit. She's waiting here out of harm's way until you can manage to control yourself."

"Ah, she knows I'd never hurt her, don't you, little girl?—See. She's telling you herself." He picked the hen up and at the same time fished a small peppermint ball from one of his belt pouches. This he put on the table and proceeded to shatter it with a sharp tap from the handle of his knife. "There. Those pieces should be about bite-size for a gurry."

"Jake!"

"Power down, Islaen! We haven't seen her for a while. She's entitled to a present."

Yes!

The Colonel gave up. "No more, then. Varn does a good enough job of ruining her without help from you."

Since she was on the outside, Islaen slipped into the galley again and produced a fresh batch of jakek. After distributing it, she sat down with a sigh. "You've found a nice bag of wrigglers for us, Jake Karmikel."

"The old man discovered something?" he inquired.

"Enough to send us here on all burners." She told him about the Alpha Gary theft and described their interview with Abana Janst.

"So there could or couldn't be a revolution that might or might not be complicated by stolen Navy weapons, though you now consider the latter to be unlikely?"

"That's just about the way it stands at the moment," she admitted.

The redhead leaned back, clasping his hands behind his neck. "Well, you'll have a crack at trying your X-ray mind out on Commissar Strombol tomorrow. You might find out something then. For now, though, let's just forget trouble for a few hours. I suggest a quick tour of the city and then a trip down to the beach once the evening's well advanced." He grimaced. "Then and early morning are the only times it's reasonable to use it anyway."

"Oh, Jake!" Islaen exclaimed in dismay. "You didn't get fried again? You know tropical suns and Noreenan skin don't mix well."

"He should know it," Bethe Danlo snorted, "but he seems to lose all his vaunted Commando survival instinct the moment he starts a furlough. I had to put him under the port's renewer our first three days on-world. —You brought our hand one, didn't you?"

"Aye, of course."

The ray was one of medicine's greatest discoveries, providing almost instantaneous, complete regeneration of damaged or destroyed skin, muscles, blood vessels, even nerves and bone. Only the organs of the chest and abdominal cavities could not be so repaired, requiring treatment with the much newer and far more complex regrowth equipment.

At the War's beginning, only a few of the great experimental hospitals could support the then-massive renewer systems, but development had progressed quickly until they became standard equipment on every major battleship, and then on the medium- and many of the smaller-class vessels as well. Now

Federation scientists had produced a model portable enough to
be used by individuals or small, mobile parties such as her unit,
which was one of the first teams chosen to benefit from and test
it in the field.

Every spaceport was outfitted with hospital-standard renew-
ers, but this one had regrowth equipment as well despite its size
and general insignificance. The fact that Tambora of Pele was
the sole Federation outpost in a large section of space made its
presence mandatory; patients requiring that kind of aid rarely
had the time left for a long voyage in search of it.

Islaen Connor smiled at Karmikel's suggestion. Tambora's
waters were reported to be warm as a tub, a welcome change
to her mind from Thorne's chilly if gloriously wild seas. Varn
would find them pathetically tame after the challenge afforded
by his adopted world's oceans, but no matter. He would benefit
as much as she from a couple of hours spent stretched out under
Pele's evening-tamed rays.

"An excellent suggestion, Comrade. I propose that we take
advantage of it as soon as possible, before something comes up
to force us into forgoing the pleasure entirely."

FOUR

ISLAEN WRIGGLED AND ran her finger under the high, tight collar of her tunic. Where was Varn anyway? They would have to be leaving for their interview with Tambora's Commissar shortly.

As if in answer to her impatience, the Commando-Captain appeared at the door of the crew's cabin.

Her eyes glowed at the sight of him. Varn Tarl Sogan looked better in a uniform than any other man she had ever seen, and he was even more magnificent in the stark black of a Federation Commando than he had been in the Empire's scarlet.

He was also the only person she had yet encountered who could not only look but actually was comfortable in a dress uniform.

The former Admiral read her irritation and laughed in his mind. *One's duty cannot always be pleasant, Colonel Connor, but do not worry. You will soon be back in your comfortable space togs again.*

You don't have to enjoy this quite so thoroughly, blast you! she muttered sourly.

Sogan only laughed again, but there was a pleasure in him that he was hard-pressed to conceal. He knew Islaen Connor liked to see him thus, and he enjoyed looking good in this woman's eyes.

Bandit fluttered to the Noreenan's shoulder. *Bandit will come?*

"Of course, love, but don't push yourself too much until we get a feel for Strombol. We don't know yet how he, or Tamborans as a whole, responds to small creatures."

Bandit will be careful! she promised.

That was no idle assurance. The Jadite creature had been part of the Commando unit long enough to be aware of the contribution her gifts could make to it and to appreciate equally well the potential consequences of carelessness or error on the part of any one of them.

"We know that, small one," Sogan told her. "You are better in that respect than any of the rest of us."

He glanced at his consort. *Ready, Islaen? We should leave ourselves good time in case they delay in admitting us.*

I was only waiting for you, Admiral.

It was a fine, bright morning, and the off-worlders paused at the top of the boarding ramp to admire the scene around them before going down to the flier Varn had readied earlier.

Sogan's eyes went to the vast expanse of the ocean, now glittering gloriously in Pele's early light, and he felt a tug of longing in his heart. Their home on Thorne stood above the sea, a wild, cold sea very different from Tambora's and yet still akin . . .

His mind abruptly snapped back to the present as Islaen's hands closed on his arm. He turned to find her body rigid and her face showing surprise and a concern that radiated even more strongly from her mind.

It was the mountain that held her, or, rather, the thick mist hovering around and just above the peak.

The man started to reassure her by suggesting that either clouds or fog must often shroud it in this tropical climate, but he stopped himself. Neither looked to be responsible for this.

He darted back inside the *Maid* and returned a few minutes later with distance lenses.

Varn raised them to his eyes, quickly focusing on the Dragon's peak.

"Spirit of Space!" he hissed aloud.

The cloud had not come to the Dragon; it was rising from it, out of it. Two, three fumaroles very near the crest were clearly visible under high magnification, and out of these, the vapor was issuing.

So it had been sulfur he had smelled yesterday, then, but he had apparently wronged the *Rounder*'s crew in laying responsibility for its release on them.

What is that stuff? he asked as he handed the lenses to his companion.

Steam most probably, the Colonel replied grimly.

Sogan turned his attention from the Dragon to the spaceport and then to the city.

No one seems to be very excited, he said at last. *Come on. It will make a poor impression if we keep Commissar Strombol waiting. We can try to question him about his mountain during our interview. By all we hear, we are not likely to get a second chance.*

Islaen Connor felt several pairs of eyes fix on them as they came down the ramp and sent her mind out.

There was some uncertainty in the touches she received— few space hounds working this backwater segment of the rim could be expected to unreservedly welcome a visit by any service brass—but mostly, there was just mild curiosity. Strangers were in themselves a rarity to Tambora's spaceport, much less strangers who wore the dress uniform of Commando officers.

Her head raised in pride, however, when the eyes of the Patrol-Yeoman at the exit widened as he waved them through. The Navy was not generous in distributing even its decorations. Citations were rarer still, and few people had seen the famed star of a heroism citation, first class. Five of them glittered on her left breast, six on Varn Tarl Sogan's.

Six. Visnu. Astarte. Jade. Mirelle. Omrai. Anath.—In the short period of time since their chance meeting on Visnu of Brahmin, this valiant, compassionate former enemy had risen to become the Federation's most highly honored soldier.

She shivered then in her soul. Every one of those bright stars bore witness to how often he had faced, aye, and well-nigh courted death for the sake of the peoples it had become his duty to guard. Every one of them was a reminder of how often and how closely she had come to losing him.

The flier soon entered the outskirts of Strombolis and began working its way carefully along the narrow streets, which already showed heavy pedestrian traffic despite the early hour.

It was a bustling scene and a rather gay one. Tamborans loved color, at least in their dress. The brighter blues and greens, yellows, reds, and oranges were everywhere to be seen. Only the purples seemed not to be represented. Either suitable dyes were not available or the connotation of luxury and the exotic made them unacceptable.

Each person wore but one shade, without pattern or any mixing even of tone in the garments, which were severely practical in cut and were fashioned out of common, heavy-duty materials.

The Tamborans themselves formed a striking contrast to their brilliant clothing. They were absolutely monochromatic. Skin, hair on head and face, and even eyes and lips were all of precisely the same shade, that of the sand on an average Terran beach, so that, if seen quickly and at a distance, they could appear as if they had no features at all.

They were a small people, stocky of build with flat or somewhat dished faces. The forehead and cheeks were broad, the nose a bare rise in the general oval of the head. The mouth was quite large with proportionally heavy lips. These were also pressed firmly to the flesh surrounding them. The eyes were perfectly round and small and seemed smaller still by reason of their lack of contrast with their setting. The women wore their hair a trifle longer than did the men; children were miniatures of the adults.

There were relatively few youngsters. Tamborans were a long-lived, healthy race with little land available to support them, and conception was permitted only to maintain current population levels. The other islands would have more little ones at present to compensate for those sent into the Navy during the War and slain or subsequently banished, but Strombolis' populace, with its specialized administrative skills and those providing the equally essential support services, had been spared from the planet-wide draft almost completely.

The simple, attractive buildings were set very close to one another, but because they were well designed, they did not seem crowded.

Most of them were dwellings. Each family unit was expected to be well-nigh self-sufficient, and there were very few goods or services that they could not supply for themselves. The rare shops that did exist catered mainly to the needs of the administrative workers, whose duties prevented them from engaging in the labors occupying the most of their race.

The proprietors of these shops received payment in goods or service. Tambora had no currency of her own, and the use of Federation credits was forbidden since specie was viewed as the core of a great part of the galaxy's evils.

Islaen peered into yet another of the small display windows as they sped past it and sighed.

There was something in the sound that made her companion look away from the controls. *What is troubling you, my Islaen?*

Strombolis. Tambora. This is the saddest place I've ever visited.

She is a beautiful world! the Arcturian protested in amazement, *and the city is well enough planned not to be a blight on her.*

Aye, the planet supplies inspiration in plenty, but her people are so fearful of developing anything others might desire, anything at all that might draw the interest of off-worlders, that they have become a race dedicated to mediocrity. —What a betrayal of the human spirit! What infinite tragedy . . .

He studied her downcast features for a few seconds before returning his attention to his vehicle. *You are right, my Islaen,* he said thoughtfully. *It is a tragedy, one I wish that we might change.*

We can't. They have become what they are by their own choice. Tamborans have a right to their own ways, but I, for one, thank the Spirit of Space for the richness of experience our own worlds have given us as our birthright.

As the flier penetrated into the heart of the city, it passed several groups of scarlet-robed individuals. Red Ascetics.

Both eyed them curiously. The vividly clad clerics represented the strongest political and moral force on the planet. It was they who had charge of the people's spiritual development and they who educated the children. Each youth, upon the completion of his or her education, entered into service at one of the monasteries for two years for training in meditation and the other skills helpful in acquiring knowledge of self and the peace of mind and spirit so valued by their society.

It was a rewarding experience, apparently, for many stayed several years longer or, in the case of some of the males, permanently joined the community, and nearly everyone returned for intervals of a few days to several weeks now and then when the need to renew their inner life came upon them.

Only once did the off-worlders see any of the much-less-common Gray Ascetics, two men walking together who turned their faces away at their first sight of the machine.

Their uncharacteristically somber-hued robes gave them a somewhat sinister look. Sogan knew that the impression was not entirely mirrored in fact but scowled at them all the same, recalling all he had learned of their kind.

The two were part of the only formal remnant of the ancient sect that had been responsible for the settlement of Tambora. As such, it exercised an influence far beyond its actual numerical strength.

That emotional power was unfortunate, he thought, for instead of the tranquillity that was the goal of their red-clad counterparts, these ones sought isolation, complete isolation, for Tambora's offspring and regarded all other intelligent life with a mistrust that bordered on paranoia. They had put off their bright orange robes for this dull gray on the day the popular vote had formalized the planet's fellowship with the Federation, and when their efforts to block the subsequent continuation of the spaceport had also failed, they had turned to striving to limit off-worlders entirely to its precincts.

In this, too, they had been foiled. The populace was not cruel and had been unwilling to fashion what amounted to a gigantic prison to confine people guilty of no actual crime or, indeed, to restrict the strangers at all beyond what was deemed necessary for Tambora's safety and well-being.

The measures they believed to be required were harsh enough and were in a large part due to the work of the gray-garbed brotherhood, as was the attitude against which Abana Janst had railed. Were this a race more prone to violence or had the rest of the Gray Robes' policies not so quickly proven disastrous to the then-young colony, they could have been deadly opponents.

He scowled again. Trouble might still come from them, trouble for their own kind, trouble for the spaceport, trouble for his comrades and for him.

The war prince's mouth twisted. He despised these people. Nearly everything he had heard about them, even most of the supposed virtues other Federation citizens were willing to ascribe to them, served only to deepen his contempt for them.

As for the Tamborans themselves, the taped images of them that he had studied had told him what to expect, but still the very sight of them made him want to retch. It once would have been inconceivable to imagine such creatures being permitted into his presence, being permitted to exist at all.

He stopped himself, disgusted at the turn of his own thoughts. He had thrown all of worth in his life away because he had refused to obliterate Thorne of Brandine and all the life she supported. Was this any better, willing within himself the annihilation of a people even if he no longer had the power to have it done in fact? Was he reverting to that mind-set despite all he had learned in his new life?

A wave of frigid anger lashed him, and he realized that he had been broadcasting all his distaste for those around them, although the thoughts and doubts accompanying it had remained well hidden in his inner mind.

His head snapped toward his companion and found her glaring at him in wordless fury. *You were not so dispassionate yourself on Anath when we encountered your people's old foes!* he snarled.

The Noreenan stiffened as though she had been struck. "No, I wasn't," she snapped, abruptly switching to verbal speech as her own shields severed him from her thoughts, "but I didn't violate our mission or endanger it. See that the same can be said of you here."

Sogan bit back the retort that sprang to his iips. He had not realized that was so sore a nerve with her. "I am sorry, Islaen," he said quietly.

"Forget it," she told him coldly.

"Islaen . . ."

Her eyes fixed on the windshield. "That's the place we want up ahead."

FIVE

THE FLIER SKIMMED across the humped-back bridge spanning the stream that neatly bisected the city and sped toward the now clearly visible palace.

The building was yellow in color and very large by Strombolis' standards. Only a relatively small part of it was devoted to the Commissar's personal use, however, the rest being given over to office space, record storage, and other needs of the many functions coming under the auspices of the island's and the planet's highest official.

Two orange-clad men straightened as the off-worlders left their vehicle and approached the door. Neither gave salute, a gesture alien to a planet possessing no military organization, but they promptly ushered the pair inside, where a solemn-faced woman wearing the same livery took charge of them. She escorted them through a fairly bewildering tangle of corridors until at last they came to a door stenciled with the Commissar's title. His name was not shown.

"Ye are expected," she said in the excellent if archaic Basic that was the language brought to Tambora by her first-ship colonists and inherited by their descendents.

The woman left them abruptly after telling them to enter about thirty seconds after knocking.

Islaen rapped sharply on the plain surface, then glanced once at Varn. She linked her mind receptors with his so that he would also be able to read their presumably unwilling host's transmissions.

Sogan opened the door for her. The room into which they came was large and airy and was simply but most adequately

furnished. Its sole occupant had apparently been seated behind
the huge, ledger-strewn desk but had risen at the sound of their
knock. He looked to be in his race's early middle years as
nearly as they could judge and was unremarkable in appearance
save that he bore himself with the unmistakable air of one born
to command.

So he had been. The position of Commissar came through
inheritance, and Ivan Strombol was direct heir and name-son to
the first man to hold the title, he who had assumed it after the
disintegration of the Orange Ascetics' temporal power.

The Tamboran greeted the off-worlders and thanked them
for the quick and safe delivery of the serum.

Seeming but to continue with the formal courtesies required
by diplomacy, he went on smoothly, "I am unfamiliar with
your people's customs, Colonel Connor, and so I cannot help
wondering if officers of your rank always carry out such minor
errands or whether Tambora has been singularly honored for
some reason."

Careful, Islaen! her consort warned.

I know, friend. The Noreenan had not missed the fact that no
welcome had been included in the on-worlder's greeting, and
she was aware of the fact that the children of the Commissars,
those who would themselves someday rule, traditionally received part of their education from the Gray Ascetics. This
man was no friend even if he was not an actual enemy, as the
readings she was receiving from him all too vividly proclaimed. "A medical run is always regarded very seriously, sir,
but, no, Captain Sogan and I should not normally have been
chosen to make this one."

She went on to describe their relationship with the two
guerrillas already on-world and explained that both she and her
superiors had decided Tambora was the perfect site to cap their
furlough, whose uncommon length had been dictated by their
physician's command.

"I hope ye will find quick healing, then," the Tamboran
leader told her without enthusiasm.

He recognized his lack of courtesy in that response and felt
the need to offer some excuse for it. "I must be frank with you,
Colonel. We are not happy with the number of aliens whose
presence we are forced to endure, and your profession,
however necessary ye deem it to be, is particularly repugnant

to us. Unfortunately, as with many evil and banned things, there is a mystique about it which might lure some inexperienced and impetuous souls. We cannot and shall not risk having our people, our young, corrupted, led into strange, wild ways."

"That's never happened before, sir, and Federation soldiers, including many Commandos, were invalided on Tambora during the course of the War. It should be no different now, particularly since Captain Sogan and I do prefer to keep to our own company and that of our close comrades."

Varn Tarl Sogan's eyes slitted. He kept his anger under tight rein, but he could feel it burning within him, an unpleasant scalding in breast and mind.

How dare this creature speak so to her? Tambora of Pele was no paradise of the old gods that merely to be here was a privilege in itself, to be merited and earned at high cost, nor was an interview with her people's leader so mighty an honor, whatever the Commissar himself might believe to the contrary.

Strombol apparently found this audience distasteful, demeaning, but the former Admiral felt little pity for him on that account. He himself was enduring far worse. His own loathing and sense of defilement were so powerful that he had to fight himself to keep from openly fleeing the big chamber and the man poisoning its very atmosphere. If he could stand against that, if he could recognize and challenge the conditioning that was drawing it forth, he could find little sympathy in his heart and less patience for a man who would not examine the conclusions born of a similar, equally faulty base and do battle with those his reason had to declare unsound.

He said nothing, however. Control was expected of a war prince of the Arcturian Empire. Besides, he had just conceived an idea that might prove useful to them.

All this while, Bandit had hung back in compliance with her orders, concealing herself behind the tall back of a chair and pouring out her power to soften the Tamboran so that he would at least not turn on her humans in open hostility, perhaps confining them entirely to the spaceport as he had more than half planned to do.

Sogan now called the gurry to come forward, to perch on his shoulder.

"We hope to be ready to leave very shortly ourselves,

Commissar. One grows extremely weary of having his energies and strength perpetually at low power.

"We have no wish to give unintended offense while we are Tambora's guests and would like to have your judgment regarding our nonhuman comrade. We are uncertain how much liberty we may give her since we were unable to find any information describing Tamboran feelings about such small creatures."

As he spoke, Bandit peered at the Commissar with great apparent interest, cocking her head, first to one side, then to the other, and purring in a show of pleasure and contentment Sogan knew she did not feel. She, too, could receive their host's thoughts and was well aware that he was no friend of her companions and that the meeting could all too readily turn sour to the disadvantage of their mission.

Whatever his opinion of Federation guerrillas, Ivan Strombol was no more immune to the little mammal's charm than most of the rest of his species. His face softened until it was almost pleasant even to the Arcturian, and he restrained himself only with difficulty from reaching out to stroke her. "My people are fond of small animal life," he told them, "both many of the species native to Tambora and those which we originally brought with us. We would find nothing offensive in her."

"Good. Bandit is well behaved, as you can observe, but she is winged and does enjoy ranging the sky occasionally. We should hate to have to keep her confined."

"There will be no need for that. The little beast will find ready welcome wherever she goes on Tambora. She is not responsible for human error, after all."

A suddenly recognized possibility caused his expression and thoughts to darken. "Unless ye plan to try importing her kind, to use her to create a market for them as pets."

"There's no fear of that, sir," Islaen assured him. "Jade's people guard her gurries jealously and will allow none save this one to be taken off-world."

"Ye forced that exception?"

The Commando-Colonel gave some of her annoyance rein. "You overstep yourself, Commissar! —They permitted it because she had grown so attached to us and we to her that to sever us would be a cruelty and because we had twice saved the colonists from utter destruction, on each occasion at great peril to ourselves."

"My apologies, Colonel Connor," Strombol said after a moment. "I knew no wrong against ye that I should have imputed that to ye. —The-gurry is quite a delightful little beast and will be well received anywhere she flies."

"Thank you. That's a relief to us." Her mind touched Varn's. *That turned out very well, but why did you bring it up in the first place?*

I wanted to know how closely she will have to guard herself if we decide to send her out scouting. With Bandit perched in the rafters and linked to me, even the Gray Robes' conferences would be open to us.

She served us well in that capacity on Anath, Islaen agreed. Her tone lightened. *You're developing a very devious mind, Admiral Sogan.*

That is inevitable considering the company I have been keeping, Colonel.

It was apparent that the audience was drawing to an end. The Noreenan thanked Ivan for the time he had given them, but she hesitated before taking her leave of him.

"May I impose upon you further, Commissar Strombol, though I readily admit my concern is the product of my own weakness and nothing based upon real cause?"

"Of course, Colonel," the Tamboran replied a bit pompously.

"Commandos have had to contend with some very seismically active planets. As a result, we're all nervous of anything that looks even remotely like it might be getting ready to go off."

"Oh, you mean the Dragon?"

Islaen could feel the superiority swelling in him. "Aye," she replied meekly.

"Ye need not fear that. It is quite extinct, as are all Tambora's volcanoes. In fact, ye are present at a very rare spectacle, though," he added as the courtesy suddenly suggested itself to him, "it must seem very little to people of your background. Only twice before, once in each of the last two centuries, have we had any such display."

He paused. "The last time, over one hundred years ago, there was an ashfall as well. The Red Ascetics collected a

goodly amount of the discharge in commemoration of the event
and have preserved it in several of their monasteries. Ye may
not visit any of them, of course, but I shall request that a small
amount be delivered to ye at the spaceport so that ye may
assure yourselves of its harmlessness."

The woman thanked him warmly, for she knew this was,
indeed, an extraordinary gesture on the Commissar's part and
one she believed to be sparked by a genuine desire to relieve
her worry. Abana had told them that these people were not
cruel, but she realized now that they were actively kind when
their fears permitted them to be.

SIX

THE SAME WOMAN who had guided the Commandos to the office was waiting to take them back. She was as stern-looking as she had been upon their arrival, and if she was surprised by the length of the meeting, she gave no sign of it in word or gesture. Both off-worlders were well glad to reach the outer door and be free of her company once more.

Varn Tarl Sogan took the controls of the flier again and made no delay in bringing them away from the palace.

You handled that extremely well, he told his companion as they passed over the little bridge.

Thanks, she replied wearily. *Diplomacy may have its place in our profession, but I'm sure as space glad I don't have to work that hard every time we have to deal with some planet hugger. I feel like I've spent the morning slinging cargo.*

He made her no answer, and when she glanced at him, she thought he seemed even grimmer than he had been on their journey to the palace. *What's wrong now?*

I did not enjoy watching you make little of yourself in there, he told her tightly.

But I didn't! It was no hurt to me to feed the Commissar's sense of superiority. As for admitting to nervousness about volcanoes, that's no more than the truth. It certainly is with respect to the Dragon.

Strombol said it is safe.

Aye, that's what he said.

He nodded but did not speak again, and a heavy silence fell between them.

Islaen watched Sogan awhile. He was looking straight

49

ahead, his gaze so seemingly distant that she momentarily
wished that it were she who held the controls. The streets
around them were narrow and crowded and required the full
attention of the driver of even an airborne vehicle moving at
this slow rate.

She forced herself to relax. Varn had proven more than once
that a preoccupied appearance was no indication of anything
wanting in his alertness to his surroundings.

He seemed only to tighten as the minutes passed, and she
started to frown. How dare he refuse to so much as look at the
people around them, as if they were nothing or, worse,
abominations to human life?

She gripped her temper. She might detest this part of him,
but she knew that it could be powerful enough to physically
sicken him. It might be something more basic than moral
revulsion and his fear of provoking her response to it that was
holding him so quiet. "We could stop for a bit," she suggested,
aloud because she did not want to disrupt what could be a
tenuous command over his body.

"No," he replied, flushing slightly. He recognized what she
was thinking and knew that he did not even have a real right to
anger because she had misjudged him on this occasion. He had
merited no better too many other items. "I am all right."

Nooo! the gurry protested from her perch on the seat back
between them. *Varn is worried!*

He scowled at her, and Bandit subsided unhappily, recalling
too late how much he disliked having inner thoughts broadcast
that he had purposely or subconsciously closed because he
regarded them as marks of weakness.

Sogan sighed in his heart. He would now be able to justify
himself before Islaen, but it would be at the cost of appearing
a coward in her eyes.

*I was thinking about that mountain—What do you know
about such phenomena, Islaen? We do not have to contend with
the like on the Empire's worlds, and I am almost completely
ignorant of their workings.*

I'm little better, she confessed, then continued thoughtfully,
*You make a good point, Varn. I'll requisition some specific
details. It can't hurt us at all to become a bit more knowledge-
able on the subject since we're going to have to live and work
in that thing's shadow until we've finished up on Tambora.*

* * *

The pair were not back aboard their starship more than a few minutes before Jake and Bethe joined them to hear the Colonel's report of the meeting.

"That was a smart move putting the lights on Bandit," the demolitions expert said when the other woman had finished. "Even a Tamboran's human enough to melt a bit around her."

"Strombol was less cold to us after that," Islaen Connor agreed. "That's what gave me the opening to ask about the Dragon."

"His answers were real helpful," Karmikel commented sarcastically. "Well, maybe those ashes will tell us something if he keeps his word about sending us a sample."

"He'll keep it," she told him.

The Noreenan man frowned. "I may be no more a volcanologist than our feathered friend here, but I'm still not dim enough to believe that a volcano that spits steam and ash is extinct, even if it does shake itself only once every hundred years or so. That Dragon up there may have been asleep, but it's stirring now, and I don't like at all that there's no one on this hole of a planet, no one, who can tell us how far it's likely to come to waking for a fact."

Islaen's lips pursed. "Maybe there is, or was," she said slowly after a moment's thought.

Her eyes flickered from Karmikel to the blond spacer. "You two have been on-world some time now, and Commandos are notoriously curious. It wouldn't be out of character for you to forgo some of your remaining beach time to go over the Tamboran public archives to learn what you could about her and her people before you have to leave and lose the chance entirely.

"Do that. Keep a look out for any hidden hint of volcanic activity you can find—unexplained crop failures or wildlife migrations, increased death rates or a sudden rise in demand on medical facilities, particularly from outside a given region, unusual fauna behavior, changes in the sea, mention of any actual action such as Strombol described today, anything at all unusual that might conceivably be of geophysical origin."

Her brows came together in a deep frown. "That man wasn't trying to deceive us this morning. He'd have given us a better story if he were. I think he fully believed every word of that

contradictory assurance. It's to himself that he was lying. All
the populace has been doing that, maybe from the time they
first shipped down here, and if that's the case, it may not be an
easy task to find what we're seeking, if any trace of it has been
recorded at all."

"You're riding a comet's tail, Islaen," Karmikel told her.
"Tambora's citizens may not be an appealing lot, but don't try
to tell us that this is a planet of total vacuum brains . . ."

"That, no," Varn Tarl Sogan answered for her, "but I think
she has read it right. The core of their existence appears to be
their need to avoid interaction with the rest of the Federation.
If they ever allow themselves to acknowledge that their world
may be seismically alive after all, they would be compelled to
bring in scientists to study her. Failure to do so would be a
gross endangering of life totally at variance to the ethic they
profess. The only way they can avoid having to make that
choice is by blinding themselves completely to even the
possibility of peril from Tambora's heart."

He drew a deep breath as an icy chill suddenly rippled
through his innermost being.

"I, for one, hope they are right and that we need face nothing
more than Tamboran revolutionaries, not that terrible thing
towering above us all."

SEVEN

ISLAEN SLEPT LATER than usual the following morning, and her consort was lingering over the last of his jakek when she at last came into the crew's cabin.

She started for the minute, well-equipped galley, but Varn waved her into her usual place. *Sit. I have the range programmed.—Syntheggs will be all right?*

Fine.

The Arcturian waited until the food and inevitable jakek were ready, then returned to the table and set them before her. He brought a few crumbs of sweet cake as well, desert for the seemingly ever-hungry gurry, who had taken a full breakfast with him.

He did not interrupt the woman while she was eating. It was a nearly universal custom among those who ranged the starlanes to attend to their food quickly and in relative silence, a habit born of the suddenness with which an emergency could arise to abruptly terminate a meal. Only when she had settled back with her jakek did he speak again.

What is our agenda for today, Colonel?

Oh, it's still early enough for a quick dip before Pele gets too hot. After that, we get down to business. We should start touring the island, I suppose. We need to have a proper feel for it before we can hope to detect anything out of the norm . . .

Her head turned sharply toward the entrance as she picked up Bethe Danlo's familiar mind pattern. The Sergeant was coming fast and in considerable excitement.

The spacer burst into the cabin a few moments later.

"Commissar Strombol can save himself the trouble of

sending us ash samples!" she told them, holding up her hand to
display a coating of pale gray-white dust.

The other two leaped to their feet. Sogan caught her wrist,
wrenching it back so sharply that she gave an involuntary gasp.

The stuff was nearly as fine as Lir talc and was unmistakably
ash, although he instinctively glanced at Islaen for confirmation.

She nodded but said nothing as she whirled for the main
hatch. Her comrades followed in the next instant.

All three stood silent while they surveyed the world before
them, a different one from that which had greeted them the
previous morning. Now, everything was covered by a fine
dusting of gray, as if a particularly dingy snow had fallen
during the night. The areas where the starship crews and the
port maintenance people had already begun the tedious cleanup
stood out in sharp contrast to the rest.

The Arcturian's hand whitened as his grasp on the railing
tightened. "By the Empire's gods!" he muttered aloud. His
thoughts he kept firmly closed.

Islaen Connor glanced up at him. *Strombol said the Dragon's done this before. No harm came of it then.*

He gave her a strange look. *Are you trying to comfort me or
yourself?* he asked.

Both. She shivered despite the morning's heat. "When did
this happen, Bethe?"

"Sometime in the wee hours. Jake and I just discovered it
ourselves."

"Where is Karmikel?" the former Admiral inquired.

"Over there, scrubbing the *Moon.*" She sighed. "Everyone
in the port'll be doing that for the rest of the day. This stuff's
a misery to take off." Her eyes went to the Commando-
Colonel. "What're we going to do, Islaen?"

"We have to get help. I don't know enough to handle this."

"Federation volcanologists?"

"Aye.—I'll put the call through on scramble as soon as we
go back inside."

"Why scramble?" her husband asked in surprise.

"I don't know, really. A feeling. I'd just prefer to keep my
activities with respect to this as quiet as possible. Tamborans
appear to be very sensitive of any sort of criticism, which
would seem to include official doubt about the stability of their

pet volcano. I don't want to start any intraFederation incidents, and I may need the locals' cooperation later. I have little enough chance of securing much of that as it is without openly antagonizing them at this stage."

"You'll wind up doing that anyway if this doesn't fizzle out," Bethe predicted glumly.

"I know, but there's no use starting out by letting them know I'm calling for the very inquiry they've emphatically refused to permit so often in the past."

"She is right as usual," Sogan said. "We do have to play this carefully, however much we need information."

He paused. "Before you make any report, though, Islaen, remember that this will probably amount to nothing. It might do more harm than good if you were to make too much of the Dragon's stirring on your first call."

"Don't worry. I intend to tell what I've seen and the little I've learned and let the experts give me the answers, or at least some possibilities."

The woman's shoulders straightened, and she glared at the ash still clinging to the usually spotless starship. "You'd best start on the *Maid*, Varn. I'll join you as soon as I'm done transmitting."

"Aye. —Set the energy pickets while you are on the bridge. That will keep any more of this stuff off her. I do not want to face another job like this tomorrow morning."

The Noreenan nodded. "Maybe we'd better activate her stabilizers as well. She's pretty steady, but you can never tell."

"Good thought. Go to it now, and hurry back out. There will be plenty left for you to do."

"That's a reminder that I should be getting back to help poor Jake," Bethe announced. "We'll set our pickets and stabilizers as well." She gave a disgusted shake of her head as she looked again at the gray dust marring the spaceport and its ships. "Maybe we'll see the three of you tonight in the Spinning Star?"

"Perhaps. We'll all be wanting a change of scene after this day's work."

Islaen turned to go inside once the spacer left them, but a piercing whistle from Bandit stopped her. "What's the matter, love?"

Bandit can't help Islaen and Varn here! Start scouting instead?

The woman hesitated as she looked down at the ash-strewn planting field. Everything did seem quiet now . . .

"All right, Bandit, but be very careful."

Bandit's always careful!

"I know, love, but this time, you'll have to watch out for the Dragon as well as for renegade humans."

She paused to collect her thoughts. "Go to the palace and around the city first. I'm as interested in the reaction to the ashfall, if there is one, as in anything else right now. Then check out the various monasteries. All this may spark enough excitement to cause revelations of one sort or another."

Yes, Islaen!

"Don't try to do it all at once," she warned. "You'll probably have to visit our biggest suspects again and again, and we'll all have to scour the island and study the dwellings and farms outside the city closely. This first flight really will be just, a run-through for you."

Bandit understands!

The gurry's head turned from side to side, looking from the city to the bright, calm ocean. *Tambora's pretty! People ugly!*

Varn Tarl Sogan looked at her sharply, a sick horror filling his soul. Had he infected her, poisoned her clean, curious mind with his inbred darkness?

He made himself relax. She had probably only been referring to the basic unfriendliness of their reception at the palace and to all she had overheard concerning this race.

"Maybe, but they are our responsibility all the same. —Fly now, small one, and take care as Islaen told you."

Yes, Varn!

He watched her until her tiny form disappeared from view, then turned away. *I had best start on the* Maid, he said stiffly.

She'll be all right, Varn. There's nothing stupid or careless about Bandit.

Aye, but it rankles me to send her off alone to do the company's work. We may have a hard day ahead of us, but we will not be facing danger. She could if fortune goes against her.

She's a member of the unit, too, Islaen Connor reminded

him, *and she has proven capable of guarding herself. We'll just have to trust her now.*

He nodded, but the auburn-haired woman sensed a deeper trouble on him. Her mind reached out tentatively to him but found his closed against her.

There was no point in trying to force a revelation from him, nor had she the right to attempt to do so. The very fact that they could share thought carried with it the powerful obligation to strictly respect the sovereignty and basic privacy of those thoughts.

She sighed in her heart, accepting her defeat as she had been forced to accept it so often before on similar occasions.

This time, however, he stopped her. *Islaen?*

Aye? She could feel the uncertainty in him, although he strove to minimize the extent of it.

Do you believe Bandit can take-attitudes from us?

The woman's eyes closed. He carried enough guilt about his inability to accept the Federation's more physically divergent citizens as it was, and this new dimension of it must be a knife through him.

She schooled herself carefully to reveal no sign of what she was feeling for him. *No. She is without question the fairest and clearest-minded being I've ever encountered. She may be a bit more cautious than usual with people we don't like or trust for one reason or another, but that's about as far as it goes. Enemies and renegades, she understands, but she can't make any sense at all out of our less logical distastes.*

EIGHT

ISLAEN CONNOR STUDIED her surroundings with wry amusement as she recalled the last time she had eaten away from either her headquarters or the *Fairest Maid*. The Spinning Star made a rather startling contrast to Thorne's Silken Robe.

The tavern was of one kin with all the others serving small, isolated commercial ports along the rim.

A number of tables filled the center space, and more comfortable and private booths lined most of three walls. The bar occupied the fourth. This one was not mirrored, the space behind it being put to the more practical use of storing various cylinders and vials, none of which would be likely to hold any of the refined delicacies or the rare liqueurs that were the delight of the inner-systems. The lighting was good, the floor bare. The latter was clean, as was the rest of the establishment, but unpolished, and it showed the sign of years of wear.

The bar itself was crowded although it was still early. After a day spent clearing away the tenaciously grasping ash, both the spacers and the port hands were tired and very thirsty.

The Noreenan woman had finished her meal, which she had found acceptable although by no means notable, and was leaning back in her booth, watching the flow of the crowd.

Sogan had not joined her, but she was not particularly surprised or put out. He had not promised to do so, and he really detested seafood, which was the only fare available here. She would give him a few minutes longer just to be sure he was not coming and then start out for the *Maid*. Her back and arms were aching after her uncommonly heavy labors, and she would welcome another session under the steam jets and then her bed.

The door banged open, and Islaen saw the crew of the *Rounder* push their way inside.

They were Malkites, all male, of course, since Malki's women did not work off-world.

The first impression they gave was of size. They were huge men, not extraordinarily tall although distinctly so, but showing the almost grotesque development of chest, shoulders, and the muscles of arms and legs characteristic of their race.

Their complexions were a fiery carrot red, their hair coarse and black, their eyes well spaced and dark. Features were heavy with a particularly strong beetling of the brows, which met in an arch above the nose.

The lips were thin and drew back when they spoke or laughed to reveal the most visible sign of mutation on them, the very large teeth, which were well separated and distinctly pointed. Their first-ship ancestors had quickly learned that few if any crops would grow on Malki, and if they were going to eat, it would have to be meat. Over the centuries, their bodies had adapted to that diet and to the rigorous means necessary for securing it.

Their voices were naturally harsh, and these men were not inclined to soften or lower them. Islaen winced at the decided increase in the decibel level of the room and resolved to leave as quickly as possible. The spacers had made a good start in comforting themselves for their unexpected day's labor, and she did not imagine the atmosphere would grow any quieter as the evening progressed. She had stayed long enough anyway.

Just as she was about to slide out of her seat, Zubin, the *Rounder*'s master, caught sight of her. "That's the one I want to talk to!" he roared.

His comrades seemed to try to dissuade him, but he brushed them aside and strode toward her.

The Commando sighed as she eased her blaster from its holster and glanced quickly at it to be certain the setting catch had not slipped off stun. She knew his type. There was rarely much real evil in them, and she did not want to burn the big asteroid even if he were minded to be quite nasty. If luck was with her, bravado or bluff might get her out of this without making it necessary to use the weapon at all. Bandit would be no help this time, not with all that alcohol muddling his brain.

The spacer stopped directly in front of her, as if he would cow her with his sheer bulk. "I want to talk to you."

"So you said across the room," she replied, as if with mild interest, "though you would probably prefer to talk at me."

Zubin hesitated an instant. She sensed indignation, mostly chemically fired, and a concern beneath it that was more real.

His determination returned. "Prince Sector's always been nice and quiet. You won't get rich here, but a freighter can pick up a fine little cargo now and then and bring it where it's supposed to go without minding anyone's business excepting her own. We don't need any brass nosing around to mess everything up for us."

"Perhaps you should talk about that tomorrow, when you are in some condition to enter into a discussion," an utterly cold voice advised.

The Malkite whirled about to face Varn Tarl Sogan.

Islaen's heart seemed to leap into her throat and freeze there as she watched the two men. That wall the Arcturian used to distance himself from others and the potential danger most strangers represented was an asset here: The other, accustomed to dealing with more-or-less unchecked emotion, did not know what to make of this or how to anticipate the kind of action it would spark. He was drunk, however, and uncertainty could turn him mean . . .

The Commando-Captain's eyes bore into him. "Our reasons for coming to Tambora and for remaining here are well enough known. If you have any questions, see me at Patrol headquarters in the morning." He did not want the big spacer anywhere near the interior of the *Fairest Maid*.

He glanced at the woman. "Ready to go, Islaen?"

Zubin glared at him. "You'll see me right now!" he snarled.

As he spoke, he hurled himself at Sogan. It was not a bull's rush but an attack perfected in countless dozens of encounters across half the Sectors on the rim, and it should have smashed all fight out of his much slighter opponent.

Varn anticipated it. He sidestepped lightly, slipping his foot in the other's path.

Zubin stumbled. The Arcturian's hands linked, came down on the spacer's neck in an infighter's blow that sent him crashing to the floor.

The remaining three Malkites started for him. Islaen brought her blaster to bear. Sogan was good, but she was not going to chance having him battered while she had the means to prevent it.

A sharp command froze their would-be assailants, and she lowered her weapon again with a sigh of relief. Jake Karmikel and Bethe stood in the doorway. Their blasters were trained on the three, and the redhead, at least, had set his to slay.

Karmikel hurried over to his comrades while the Sergeant kept the *Rounder*'s remaining crew covered.

"What's the trouble?" he asked, warily eyeing Zubin, who had sat up and was rather groggily looking about him, as if he did not know how he had come to be on the floor.

"No trouble, friend," Sogan replied smoothly. "Captain Zubin tripped just as he was about to return to his ship. —Give him a hand up, will you, and see him on his way. He might be a little shaken after a drop like that."

"Good enough," Jake replied with a grin; he had seen how that fall had come about.

Once they had moved out of hearing range, Islaen rose to join her consort.

"Thanks." She stroked the still-terrified gurry. "That was the last sort of trouble I expected here."

"You are both all right?" He also spoke aloud. They could not stand here in seeming silence with so many eyes still fixed on them.

"Fine, except I had the starlight scared out of me when that son of a Scythian ape went for you. He could have crushed you like a feather spore."

"If he got his hands on me," the man conceded with a trace of a smile, "but I was not about to allow that."

"So I noticed."

He looked toward the door. "The Malkites are gone now. I just hope they do not decide to cause you more trouble later on."

Her eyes danced. "I wasn't the one who decked him, remember?"

Their two comrades joined them. "They won't bother us again," Jake assured him. "Their type don't go in for back-alley assaults."

"If they do not kill you outright, you are away with it?" the former Admiral asked wearily; the diversity of reaction to be found within the Federation could be even more trying than its diversity of form at times.

"Precisely." Bethe laughed. "Seriously, though, a Malkite's more apt to like than hate a man who can throw him like that, especially one who doesn't involve the Patrol. You could have had him big for attacking a Navy officer, and Zubin knows it."

The Commandos left the Spinning Star. It was a relief to be away from its bustling, still-tense atmosphere, and they stopped for a few moments outside to enjoy the quiet and the freshness of the cooling night air.

"No more ash," Jake observed with relief.

"No." Islaen Connor shook her head. "Let's hope that there won't be more, of that or anything else. I shudder to think what a mountain like that might do to a city not even willing to recognize that it might be in danger."

Her remark caused an uncomfortable shuffling among her companions. They were not at all happy about the Dragon's behavior, and in voicing her own concern, the Colonel had crystallized theirs.

She gave them a wan smile. "That's classified for the time being, but, Jake, get to our Patrol friends in the morning. I want a listing of all port personnel as soon as possible, what their duties are, and who must remain until the very last to keep up basic minimal service."

"Aye, Colonel," he replied.

She started to speak again, but the words froze in her throat.

The ground moved beneath her feet, not much, but she could feel the vibration in her legs, and for all her space-fostered sense of balance, she reached out to Sogan for support.

Instinctively, her head snapped toward the Dragon.

There was still some ghost of a light in the sky, and as Islaen watched, a cloud shot forth from the peak, just one, but huge-looking even at this distance, as if some titanic beast had suddenly taken a dislike to the bite it had been chewing and spat it out.

It dispersed rapidly. Too rapidly. Within three minutes, less, she heard the crack of hard objects striking the paving of the planeting field.

Jake's arms swept around his companions. He shoved them

back into the slightly recessed doorway of the Spinning Star
and pushed himself in behind them.

Their shelter was too shallow to afford them full protection,
but the roof kept the falling material, some of it uncomfortably
large, off them, and the Noreenan used his body to shield the
others from ricochets skipping on the pavement near them.

There were only a few of the last, and fewer still struck
squarely, but twice he jerked in response to blows despite his
efforts to hold himself still.

The bombardment was over in a matter of seconds, and
Karmikel stepped back, releasing his comrades.

"Jake, are you hurt?" Bethe asked, her voice sharp with
concern. She had been pressed tightly against him and had felt
his response to at least two hits. The second blow had wrung
a groan from him, and she knew full well that there had to have
been more whose striking he had successfully concealed.

"A few bruises. Nothing more," Karmikel replied, realizing
there was no point in trying to deny all injury. "What about the
rest of you?"

"Nothing touched us," Islaen assured him. "Hold still a
moment, you big ape! I'm not so sure about you."

Jake nodded readily and braced himself, knowing what was
coming. This was one of the most useful aspects of his
commander's talent. Although she could not heal an injury, she
could send her mind out and examine an organism, often
detecting and diagnosing damage, even certain illnesses, of
which the victim herself was sometimes completely unaware.

A strange tingling started within him, as if sensitive, trained
fingers were probing every cell and nerve.

It was over in a few seconds. The woman looked at him
gravely. "You're a liar, Jake Karmikel. That left shoulder
blade's chipped. You'll need a session under our renewer to set
you right."

Her eyes went from one to the other of her comrades. They
were all shaken, Varn more than any of the others, she thought.
This was something beyond anything within his previous
experience. He might accept what was happening on Tambora
of Pele scientifically, intellectually, but it was inconceivable to
him on a gut level.

"The Dragon's a force to be respected," she told them all
quietly, "but not actually to be feared, not yet."

She looked around. "Let's check the tavern first and then scare up the Patrol to go over the port. I don't want anyone lying out all night with a cracked head. Once that's done, I'll issue a warning to our neighbors to activate their stabilizers."

She gave one last look around the spaceport, now rapidly filling with milling groups, and then squared her shoulders to begin the new round of work the flame mountain had thrown on them.

Although he was bone-weary, the war prince's nerves were too raw to allow him to drop off to sleep immediately, and so he lay awake, reviewing the disconcerting events of the previous twenty-four hours.

His mind snapped back to the present as Bandit tore through the door of his cabin, which he always left slightly ajar to admit her when she chose to change her sleeping quarters during the night or to quietly withdraw when he and Islaen were together.

He sat up. As was true on most starships, the *Maid*'s air temperature was lowered during the normal sleeping period, but he ignored the chill against his bare shoulders. The gurry was obviously distressed herself and had not merely come in response to any unease that he might have been broadcasting.

"You are troubled, small one. What is wrong?"

Islaen's unhappy! Varn help!

The war prince swore at himself. He had been so tied up in his own nervousness, his own dread of that thrice-accursed fire mountain, that he had failed to recognize his wife's probably equally powerful concern. As usual. Islaen Connor had given him her love, she had restored purpose to his life, and he . . . He could not even respond to her in her need.

His mind went out in search of her and soon located her on the bridge.

His lips tightened. She had felt his seeking and had endeavored to reach out to him cheerfully, but he had felt the misery, the anguish, with which she had been contending.

"Stay here, Bandit."

Throwing his robe about himself, he sped up the core ladder with the unconscious ease and speed of one who had been schooled to space and the ships that ranged it since his youth.

The Commando-Colonel was on the bridge, waiting for him since she knew that brief contact had been enough to tell him all was not well with her. She, too, had undressed for sleep and was clad in the clinging softness of a pale blue robe fashioned from thick Thornen fleece.

Her face was composed, but she was pale beyond her wont, and her eyes looked sunken and troubled.

She smiled at him. *Varn, I'm sorry to bother you like this. I just wanted to think for a little while.*

I could not sleep, either.

He came to her, held her against him. *We seem always to draw trouble on ourselves,* he said softly, then paused, groping for something to say. *I wish I were a greater help to you . . .*

No one could do more.

Her fear surged to new life within her. *I should have listened to you,* she said. *You were uneasy about the Dragon from the start, but I thought it was just a case of nerves, a reaction to your Ruling Command's failures with respect to similar forces in the past.*

I cannot read the future, Sogan responded a bit sharply. That was one possible aspect of his talent he was not willing to accept, that his natural warrior's senses were somehow enhanced to the point that he was able to recognize in advance when they faced a mission of unusual difficulty.

You haven't been wrong yet. She shuddered. *One thing for certain, sure as space is black, the Dragon is not dead.*

She looked up at him. *What are we going to do, Varn? We could try to take on a pirate fleet—we've done it before—but how can we fight a volcano? With thirty thousand helpless sheep in that city out there, we can't even run from it.*

His arms tightened around her. *We shall do what we must,* he told her almost fiercely.

Varn's tone gentled marvelously as his lips brushed the smoldering flame of her hair. *Come, my Islaen. We must face all this tomorrow, and we both will be useless if we do not get some proper sleep.*

Islaen allowed herself to accept the comfort and strength he offered, let his love for her fill all her universe.

Aye, she whispered softly, *but stay with me awhile, Varn Tarl Sogan. It's you that I need right now, more than any rest or even any guarantee of peace . . .*

NINE

ALTHOUGH IT WAS nearly dawn when the Commando-Captain had gone to his bed, Pele had scarcely finished her rising before he arrived at Patrol headquarters.

He was alone. Islaen Connor was up as well, but she had gone off with their comrades and the Stellar Patrol unit to inspect the spaceport and city. She wanted to confirm that the damage had indeed been as negligible as they believed and to learn what if any had occurred in Strombolis itself since they could be certain that no reports or even reassurances would be coming from the Commissar's palace.

The Tamborans would realize what she was doing, of course, and would not like it, but that could no longer be helped. The Dragon had closed the question of subtlety last night.

There was a knock at the door of the tiny office the Commandos had been given for their use, and Abana Janst stepped inside. "Zubin's heading this way," she told him, "and it looks like he's flaming."

Sogan sighed. He had been afraid his challenge of the previous evening would not be forgotten. That was why he had come here instead of going out with the others. No matter. The spacers would have to be faced anyway after the Dragon's tantrum last night and the measures Islaen had instituted in consequence. "Send him in when he gets here and leave us be."

"Captain . . ." she began in protest.

"That is an order, Sergeant. I cannot run from him."

"Aye, Captain. —I'll stay within call, though, just in case."

"Thanks."

The Sirenian had scarcely left him before the spacer tore through the door and stood looming over the desk. In the confines of the small room, his bulk was enough in itself to be frightening, even without that face, which was to the war prince's mind something out of raklick roar gone sour.

Zubin slammed a paper down on the metal surface with a force that set the desk rattling. "What's the meaning of this order to activate my stabilizers?" he demanded. "Do you have any idea what that would cost me long-term?"

"Not as much as raising the *Rounder* if she should be knocked off her fins," he responded calmly. "You would have to pay the charges for that service, you know, if you ignore an official warning, not to mention the cost of repairing any damage she might sustain, and you could find yourself with a very long wait before anyone would come to lift her for you."

The Malkite swelled with rage, but Varn cut him off before he could give vent to it. "Shut that door and sit down. You are neither a prisoner nor my servant."

Zubin obeyed. "What do you people want? To beggar us all?"

"That is a warning Colonel Connor sent out, not an order, and I was not threatening you just now."

"It sounded like it."

"Maybe, but I was giving you stark facts."

His eyes fixed the other. He had learned their very coldness gave them a sort of power, and that did not fail him now. Zubin remained quiet, hostile, aye, but he was listening.

"We do not expect anything worse than we had last night and maybe not even a repetition of that, but there are thirty thousand men, women, and children in that city over there, living in buildings fashioned entirely of unreinforced stone and without a single piece of heavy or light construction or excavation equipment among the lot of them. If a quake strong enough to topple starships did strike and assuming our own gear survived, what do you imagine our priorities would have to be?"

The freighter master had more experience than he wanted with both services, Navy and Stellar Patrol, albeit not before with a Commando or an officer of this rank, but not until this moment had any soldier or agent bothered to explain or give an accounting for a command. Now he sat silently for a long time.

"I'd forgotten you people are responsible for this sort of thing, too."

His heavy brows thickened even further in a deep scowl. "You won't get much cooperation from that bunch."

"We do not expect any."

"But you'd still have to help them?"

"In every way we could. In the meantime, we have to do what we can to protect them and to protect our own people."

"By trying to see that nothing much happens here in the port, at least, in case there's a big shake-up?"

He nodded. "Or to minimize the damage as much as possible."

Once more, a scowl darkened the Malkite's features. "A mountain like that can do a lot more than shake."

"Let us take one problem at a time, Captain."

Zubin paused. "More than one of us got an ugly start last night."

"If you are nervous, go easy on the drive," the Arcturian warned. "People can die if they bolt wrong."

"Or die if they don't when they should."

"That, too."

Sogan faced him steadily. "I wish I could tell you exactly what is going to happen, Captain, but I cannot at this point. We simply do not know. As likely as not, nothing serious will occur. Nothing ever has before despite similar activity, but this planet is so damned primitive that we could all find ourselves at the mercy of that volcano if luck goes against us and we do not program our navputer right. That is the way it stands now."

"Why tell me all this?" the Malkite asked suspiciously.

"It is no more than Islaen will say to the rest later on."

"None of you were doing much talking before."

"The Dragon had not exceeded its historical precedent until last night. —We know we are not dealing with fools, at least not in the port. Everyone is on edge, and you have a right to something from us. Unfortunately, as you can see, it is little enough that we have to offer."

Zubin of Malki fell quiet again. He was watching the dark-eyed man, weighing whether to trust him and at the same time wondering what insanity moved him to even consider doing so.

Suddenly he squared his shoulders. "All right, Captain

Sogan. I'll buy what you're saying. It locks into my own thinking."

Now that he was started, the Malkite plunged ahead. "I haven't been easy about that mountain since it started up, and that business last night has me real worried, but what am I supposed to do? What's any of us to do?"

He seemed to growl deep in his throat. "The *Rounder*'s been on-world two weeks now, and the rest have been sitting here even longer. None of the planters have been near any of us yet."

This time, the growl was distinctly audible. "They know they've got us, the bastards! We'll wait because there isn't much going in this part of space and won't be until the rim starts pushing out for a fact. None of the colonies are exporters yet, so they can't buy imports, either, and steady charters like we've got from Tambora almost don't exist for the like of us. I can't afford to throw it away, and neither can any of the others."

He glowered at the former Admiral. "Am I supposed to let my ship get blown to atoms to keep it?" he demanded.

Varn Tarl Sogan leaned a little forward in his chair. "You will do what you have to do. If you choose to stay longer, I promise to keep you as informed as possible about what is going on, and you can believe that we shall not continue to grope quite as blindly as we must right now. If you decide to go, now or later, my unit will back you."

The other gave a cold laugh. "You're talking breach of contract if I lift without my cargo. Your neck'd be out as far as mine if you tried to take my part."

"Not really. You did not agree to assume any extraordinary risks, did you, apart from those normally encountered during a voyage?"

"Not for what they're paying me to transport their stuff, I didn't!"

"The Dragon is a complete unknown, and you have nothing more than your own judgment to guide you in dealing with any challenge it might present. Responsibility for that lack of information lies entirely with the Tamborans since they have repeatedly refused to permit the studies necessary to acquire it, and they have no claim against you for the decisions you make regarding it. You will probably lose the charter if you lift—the

Federation cannot force anyone to hire or retain your services—but there will be no penalties to pay. Islaen has seen to that already."

Zubin stared at him. "How?"

"She had you freighters' position clarified by Federation lawyers this morning and gave testimony as to conditions here. You are covered as far as the law goes."

The big man nodded once and then a second time. "You can't survive in the starlanes by running at every shadow of trouble. There'd be no time for anything else. The *Rounder*'s staying, at least for a while. You'll have no trouble with us while we're here," he added, "and when we do lift, we'll bring off any five or six you name. She can't handle more than that, but I'll take them anywhere you want, and there won't be a charge for the service."

Sogan smiled. "No charge, but your offer has just gotten you a mercy commendation and the credits that go with it. I hope it will not come to a heroism citation, but if the situation deteriorates so far as to warrant it, we will see to it that you come in for that as well."

The Malkite's black eyes widened for just one instant. Even at lowest levels, the sum the Commando mentioned would amount to a great deal more than the *Rounder*'s master could hope to earn in a year traveling Prince Sector's starlanes, even with the winning of an odd special cargo to bolster his gains. He, at least, was going to have good cause to be glad of the Dragon's sudden display of bad temper.

It was very late, and night had full possession of Tambora's moonless sky when the guerrilla unit reassembled in their borrowed office.

The Colonel looked tired, as well she might, but she had just scored a victory, and her relief was plain to be read.

"They're solidly behind us, every one of them. I couldn't pick up anything negative at all."

"What about fear?" Karmikel asked.

"Naturally, especially with those two new ashfalls to fuel it, but nothing like earlier. Having it out in the open helps."

Bethe Danlo shook her head. "You took an awful chance, Islaen. Suppose they'd reacted differently?"

She shrugged. "Varn tried it out on Zubin this morning, but

even if I had failed, we wouldn't be in a much worse position than if I'd kept my mouth shut. We'd be contending with the same crashing morale and threatening panic. We'd probably have lost the use of the ships, but they're too small to be of much help in any event."

She pressed her hands to her eyes. "What about your own job? Did you dig up anything of interest?"

"Precious little. Apart from the two incidents Strombol mentioned, Tambora has apparently always been a perfect lady. No trouble whatsoever."

"She would start up now," she muttered. "Did you have any problems?"

"From the locals?" Bethe shook her head. "None beyond a decidedly cold reception. Our hosts are furious over what they consider to be a violation of their private business."

"It's a terrible thing to be concerned about the welfare of others, isn't it?" Islaen demanded sarcastically.

"What about your report, little Bandit?" Sogan asked.

He had received a great part of that already through the direct linking of his sense receptors with hers, but now she described for her humans the remainder of her observations, which they then summarized for the others.

It was similar to her story of the previous day. The Dragon's more violent display had caused some initial unease, but the Tamborans had soon shaken that off and appeared to regard the event as an exciting curiosity.

The gurry had concentrated most of her efforts on the various monasteries, Red and Gray, and had discovered a good bit about life within their walls.

It was basically a good one, healthy and busy, as even Sogan, who was prepared to condemn it outright, was compelled in fairness to concede. The men divided the bulk of their waking hours between labor in the extensive gardens and at the various crafts supplying their communities' needs and in meditation. Meals were ample and consisted of the same plain foods that were eaten by their fellows in the world. Sleep time was not generous but was sufficient. Existence was regimented in all its aspects, but not much more so than that of the members of many surplanetary military and police organizations, aye, and in some divisions of the Navy and the Stellar Patrol as well.

Meditation was the strangest aspect of the clerics' lives and the most difficult for the off-worlders to understand. In general terms, it followed the same regimen in both Red and Gray establishments. The goal was self-knowledge and inner peace and was achieved through private contemplation and group study, the latter being led by an experienced superior who either read or spoke to his students.

Today, the themes of the latter addresses had been almost identical as the speakers sought to ease mind and heart after the Dragon's outburst, that and reinforce Tamboran superiority by contrasting local calm with the panic supposedly rending the aliens in the spaceport.

The previous day's talks had been different, and those of the Gray Abbot were sinister enough when viewed under the light of the Commandos' fears. He had stressed the virtues of Tambora's first settlers, the virtues the Orange Ascetics had attempted to raise to planetary rule, the danger to even their partial survival posed by the continuing, corruptive influence of the off-worlders, as exemplified by the horrors those who had been forced into the Navy had witnessed and endured.

If this were indeed his subordinates' daily fare, many, enough, of those already holding strongly to such beliefs might well be worked into the emotional pitch their leader required to accomplish his political ends.

Nothing definite, nothing incriminating, had surfaced, however, and so Bandit was instructed to resume her investigation as soon as Pele was again high in Tambora's sky.

Hopefully, life would soon return to sufficient normalcy to permit her human comrades to join with her in what had been their primary mission.

Islaen's hand raised in command for silence. A moment later, a knock sounded on the door, and Abana Janst came into the room. "We're about to finish transmitting for the night, Colonel."

"Good enough. —How did it go today? Much interference?"

The Sergeant gave a quick, appreciative laugh. "So that's why you wanted us to send our records off on scramble!"

"Not quite. I do want them preserved, but I was interested in seeing if our good hosts might try jamming you."

Abana eyed Islaen. "Let them amuse themselves with us

while you took care of the real business on the *Maid*'s transceiver?"

"Did they have any success?" the Commando inquired, smiling.

"None. We got static but corrected for it easily."

"Excellent. I figured they wouldn't have anything able to bother you, not with just a surplanetary system. —Tomorrow, I want a fix on their equipment. Get positive identification. A little leverage might be useful if we have to deal with the Commissar later."

There was no smile from either woman this time. Both knew to what Islaen Connor referred, the inevitable clash that would occur if she deemed an evacuation necessary and had to declare a death-peril emergency in order to implement it.

Bethe Danlo shivered in her heart as she listened to them, although her control was powerful enough to hold her body steady. She, too, knew to what the Noreenan had referred. That prerogative of the Navy and the Patrol to assume command of a world or area of a world under severely abnormal, usually life-threatening conditions had rarely been exercised in the Federation's long history, a bare dozen times in all in its ultimate degree, when an officer took upon himself the weight of full rule, overriding and often defying surplanetary leaders.

In every case, the extreme action had been fully and terribly justified, and never had the alien control been maintained a moment longer than necessity demanded, and so each incident had become a proud part of the ultrasystem's history and legend, its participants heroes alike to the two services and to the farflung civilian populace.

None were part of recent history. Most had taken place well back in the days when star travel was slow and a planet's suitability for colonization was determined almost more by hope and prayer and the stark determination of the first shippers well-nigh marooned upon her than by any presettlement scientific study. The most recent had happened decades before the threat of the great War just past had begun to raise its ugly head. Certainly, she had never, even in the most farfetched of her daydreams, imagined ever to be involved in the like.

Would even Commando-Colonel Islaen Connor be equal to that awesome task?

Her slate eyes measured the other woman, and she nodded slowly in her own mind. Aye, the guerrilla commander could and would accept what that entailed, brave the dangers provoking and rising from it and risk the consequences an error in judgment could, would, bring down, the enormous penalty that would fall on her should her reading of the situation be wrong. —However innocent its agent's purpose, the Federation did not play the tyrant with its member planets or lightly abrogate even briefly the rights that were theirs alone.

The demolitions expert gripped herself. She was letting her imagination run with her, turn a potential problem into deadly peril. What was being done on Tambora of Pele was merely their duty, to guard Federation citizens against possible danger on- and off-world and to prepare to meet it if it did come to pass, particularly when the local population was unable or unprepared to do so. An enraged mountain was no different from a pirate armada in that respect.

As for Islaen, she was a woman, no more than that, and a dog-tired one right now like the rest of them.

The invisible distance her thoughts of a few moments before had set between them vanished with that realization, and she gave the Colonel a wan smile.

"We're all about dead-beat. Since you left the flier back at the *Maid*, I'll commandeer one of the Patrol rovers and drive us all back home. There's more ash falling, and it's a stellar job to get it off oneself."

Sogan seemed about to refuse her, and she hurried on. "You'll hardly be putting Jake and me out any, you know," she told him tartly. "We're berthed a few yards away from you."

The Captain glanced at Islaen. She looked as spent as he was himself. "Very well, Sergeant. We are both pleased to accept."

"I thought you would be," she told him as she headed for the door. "Just don't let me hear any criticism of my driving, or you'll get out and walk."

The journey was short and passed in silence as each of the company busied himself with his own thoughts.

Sogan's attention wandered to the world outside the small vehicle.

The spaceport was quiet at last. The rover's light revealed a ghostly landscape of pale gray. Even the air blended into it.

The ashfall was very fine and not terribly thick, but it had density enough to drastically reduce visibility as the lights reflected back from each minute particle. There was a good bit of it down, too, the combined legacy of the current fall and the one that had preceded it a short time before, and this now billowed up in a fine, thick cloud around the machine with each turn of its wheels, even further reducing their ability to see.

His eyes closed wearily for a moment. He was glad not to have to be out in all that.

As they drew closer to the docking bays, he could see glimmering patches of eerie-looking light to right and left. Energy pickets. The other ships had emulated the *Fairest Maid* and *Jovian Moon* and had raised theirs so that at least the vessels themselves and their immediate environs would remain free of the powder falling so steadily elsewhere.

When they reached the freighter, he gave the command that released the voice locks, and part of the barrier dimmed so that the rover could pull inside. Once it had stopped, he and his consort made no delay in leaving it.

The Arcturian rested his hand on the ash-covered door before swinging it shut. Bethe looked small and frail and very tired. "Get some sleep, Sergeant," he ordered gruffly. "We have all done what we can at this stage, and there is no point in killing ourselves altogether."

The spacer turned her fine smile on him. "I was about to suggest the same thing to you, Admiral."

She bade them both good night with that and headed for her own ship.

Islaen watched the rover's lights recede into the night.

We're fortunate in them, she said softly after a moment.

Fortunate in them, fortunate in having you in command. He glared at the night-shadowed mountain and sighed. *Perhaps the Spirit ruling space is in truth watching over Tambora and has intervened for Strombolis in its trouble.*

Let's just hope intervention of that or any other sort won't be necessary, Varn Tarl Sogan. Mild though it's been in comparison with some of the troubles we've encountered elsewhere, I've already had more alarm than I want since coming to Pele's system.

TEN

ISLAEN'S SLEEP WAS deep and heavy, so much so that it was several seconds before she responded to Bandit's incessant calling.

Once she did become aware of it, she was instantly alert. "What's wrong now?" she demanded as she swung into a sitting position.

Transceiver! Varn says message for Islaen!

"Thanks, love." —*Varn,* her mind called. *What is it?*

Awake at last, Colonel? he answered promptly from the bridge. *Your volcanologists have been transmitting on scramble for the last hour.*

Then why in the name of space . . .

He laughed. *Power down, Colonel Connor. I have it all on tape. They did not even ask to speak with you.*

The transmission had just ended when the Noreenan reached the bridge, a fact that reassured her considerably. If the situation were seen as desperate, headquarters would have insisted on a voice conference instead of just leaving recorded information.

It was some two hours later before the Commando-Colonel summoned Karmikel and Bethe Danlo.

"Well?" demanded the redhead before he had closed the door of the crew's cabin behind him. "You heard from our scientists at last?"

She nodded. "They say the Dragon's eruptive, right enough, and a distinct threat in the face of our total lack of knowledge about it, but they have no way of being able to predict what will happen. It might follow historic pattern and peter out, or it might let go."

77

She frowned slightly. "They say all this ash could be a bad sign."

"That's scarcely more than you told everyone yesterday!" Jake exclaimed in disgust.

"They can't give answers without facts, friend," Islaen reasoned, but it required no special mind talent to read her own disappointment.

"Maybe I can get them some," Varn Tarl Sogan remarked.

"How?" asked the Sergeant. "Islaen's already told them everything we know."

"By taking a look at the crater. There should be plenty of time for that today."

The spacer stared at him. "You're on a voyage to the next galaxy, Admiral Sogan."

"No, he isn't," the Colonel told her. "There hasn't been any violence, and if we're to get some answers, we're going to have to supply the data to elicit them. We're not likely to gather very much more down here for a while. —We'd best leave as soon as we can get ready."

"I will leave," Sogan corrected. "I do not need company."

"You need me," she stated flatly. "I know more about rough country than you do and could possibly see or interpret something you might miss."

Karmikel frowned. "She's right, Admiral, and right to insist that a team make the climb, but I think I should be the one to accompany her."

"No. The idea is mine. I go."

Islaen looked from one man to the other and shook her head. Neither would give way voluntarily. "It's his baby, Jake. Back off."

She turned to the Arcturian. "Well, Admiral, do you yield? No ones goes up there alone."

His scowl told her she had won even before he spoke. "I do," Sogan conceded sourly.

He glanced at her untouched jakek. "Light your burners if you are determined to come. We should get as early a start as possible."

The flier followed the line of an unpaved road upward almost until it reached the gate leading to the plantation house it served.

At last, Karmikel brought it to a stop. They could go no farther along this route without intruding upon the on-world residents. Besides, Islaen wanted to go the rest of the way on foot so that they could better study the upper slope.

His two passengers stepped out, and the Noreenan man handed them their gear, the little they had chosen to bring. There were recorders, of course, and water, which would be wanted if they found the streams they passed tainted by too much ash or by subsurface minerals seeping into their birth-springs. The Colonel had insisted upon oxygen and lightweight surplanetary rebreathers as well. They would not use either unless necessary, but even at sea level, the scent of sulfur was often strong now, and she did not want to risk getting caught in any sort of gas cloud on the slopes, or in an extremely heavy burst of the ultrafine ash, either. In volume, that stuff might wreak havoc with the lungs. It was fear of that possibility that had made them order Bandit to return to the port with Jake despite the undoubted aid she could have given them.

The redhead wished them luck and promised to try to meet them in this place upon their return if he could not spot them beginning their descent. Between clouds and steam and the frequent eruptions of ash, the crest and upper slopes were but poorly visible most of the time. They were lucky to find it clear today, and there was no reason to assume it would remain so indefinitely.

"We'll be glad of the ride," Islaen said, "but the walk down won't kill us if we have to do it."

Karmikel glowered at them both. "Don't go taking any chances up there," he growled. "I'm still not in favor of this jaunt."

"We'll be discreet," promised the woman. "I haven't stayed alive this long in our line of work by indulging in ridiculous chances."

"You didn't win the rank you have by hiding under your bunk, either."

Varn laughed. "Stop it, you two, and let us get started, or we will never finish up and be able to come home again."

"Have it your way," the other man said as he put his machine into motion. "Don't come back grumbling that you're spent."

With that, he pulled away, steering the flier with one hand while he soothed the unhappy gurry with the other.

The pair waited for a while after he had gone, gazing out upon the scene beneath them.

It was still lovely, though not as fair as would have been true before the Dragon had stirred and cast its gray pall over everything. They were very high, nearly half the way to the peak, and both Strombolis and the spaceport looked tiny and jewel-perfect, their imperfections muted by distance. The vivid blue of the sea and sky was all the more glorious with the dimming of the land's once-brilliant green.

The view up the mountain, the way they must soon go, was not so pleasing. Neither vegetation nor ash could completely conceal the steepness of the slope nor the generally rugged terrain. They would have to choose their route cautiously, or they would have to contend with fairly impressive cliffs.

If only the Tamborans were not so bloody unreasonable, the Arcturian muttered.

The rise behind the city was so gentle and smooth that schoolchildren regularly trekked up it to hold picnics and games under the crater basin, but had they gone that way, they would have been forced to lose hours detouring around the huge Red monastery and, above that, the two Gray communities, the last of their kind left on Tambora. Outsiders would find little welcome in the one, none at all in the other, and both sects would consider their arrival as a defilement of their dwellings and workplace.

Islaen nodded absently. She had been farm raised, and her eyes were on the vegetation around them.

The ash had fallen heavier up here, and slender branches and leaves were already bowing beneath the gray dust. If much more of it came down, the planters would begin to lose, and lose sharply.

May the Spirit of Space help them, she said softly.

She caught her companion's surprised look and explained what had moved her.

His own eyes fell. This was a heartbreak with which anyone bred on an agrarian world must per force identify. Once again, he had failed to recognize his consort's pain.

Perhaps it will not come to that, he said because some response was required of him.

He turned to face the mountain. *Let us get started. There is a stiff climb ahead of us.*

So it proved. The slope was steep, seventy degrees or more in some places, and the ash gave poor footing. It was slippery in itself, and it tended to mask minor surface irregularities, making some falls inevitable.

There was no need for speed on them, however, and the pair took their time, resting frequently and giving help to each other.

They quickly learned to be careful where they put their hands, gloved though they were, and to watch where they sat when they sank down during their breaks. Some of Tambora's wildlife could be even less pleasant than her human occupants.

Paramount among creatures of that sort in this place was a slender reptile some two feet in length and covered over its entire body by black, three-inch-long spines, sharply pointed and hollow, each containing a small dose of venom powerful enough to slay should several of them succeed in penetrating the skin. The fur snakes, as they were locally named, normally burrowed in the surface layer of soil and now-buried leaf litter, but the ash was light enough to offer them little impediment as long as it stayed dry, and they were traveling through it in considerable numbers, all trying to work their way farther downslope. Apparently, the wetter conditions at the crest hardened the Dragon's ejecta, making it less acceptable to them.

They were possessed of extremely low intelligence, too low for Varn to detect readily unless he was actively hunting for them to the exclusion of all else, and both were well sick of the creatures by the time they had risen to a point above most of them, but by then, the humans' excitement was such that they had little attention to spare for any mere dislike. Soon now, they would see the crater and perhaps know . . .

They worked their way diagonally along the final slope until they reached the base of the notch overlooking Strombolis. This dip in the otherwise unbroken and quite sheer lip of the crater was deep, and they would save themselves a considerable and very difficult climb by going up there.

Islaen Connor bent to the ground before they began the ascent and, after breaking the rain-formed crust with a sharp blow of her heel, scooped up a handful of ash. She immediately allowed it to run through her fingers again, back onto the disturbed ground. She frowned slightly.

Sogan had seen her do the same thing several times before and now questioned her as to why.

In answer, she held out her hand. Four small pebbles remained on the glove along with a smear of ash dust.

Scientists call these lapilli. There aren't many in any one place, but they're pretty evenly distributed at this level. They must blow out with the ash, but the force of the blasts has not been sufficient to hold them aloft, and they drop again before they can travel far.

I wonder if this happened the last time, too, or if the Dragon is showing us something new?

We've no way of knowing. There was no mention of anything heavier than ash in material Jake or Bethe read, but maybe no one even bothered to climb up so far. More likely, they wouldn't have realized what they had anyway if they'd found the stones.

The man gave one grim look at the wall looming above them and then turned toward it without making any reply. There was a dead feeling on him that he was not going to like what they would find when they at last reached its top.

Neither spoke at all during that final stage of the ascent. It was indeed a scramble, nearly perpendicular and so treacherous of footing that they were compelled to give their full attention to it, particularly the top fourth of it, which seemed to be composed of fill, the rubble of the centuries, rather than the true heartstone of the mountain.

Once they did gain the summit, the sight that met their eyes held them silent and paralyzed.

The jungle of lush vegetation was gone, crushed and smothered by the vast weight of ash covering all the interior wall.

The bottom, once brilliantly emerald, now supported a lake over 650 feet long whose steaming waters were fed by a narrow, boiling cascade pouring from an infant cone directly opposite them on the inner wall. It was small, not quite twenty feet high, and was so angled that they could almost look into its mouth.

From deep, deep below came an eerie rumbling, a constant

bubbling, as if there were a great industrial complex in full operation far down in Tambora's heart.

The Noreenan shivered as an ancient belief of her race rose up in her mind. A demon might sound so as he forged Hell's chains.

She looked quickly away, back down the mountain, but her gaze fell on the three fumaroles visible from the spaceport below. They were huge at this close range, and a thin line of steam rose from each. It was from these, she knew, that the ever-present sulfur was issuing.

Sogan, too, was watching them somberly. *It is not going to stop, is it?* he asked without looking at his companion. *The Dragon is going to blow and blow big?*

No, it won't stop, but as for how bad the climax will be or when it will come . . .

He turned to her. There was weariness on him and a nearly infinite weight. *What are we going to have to face? Can you make any guess?*

That depends on the Dragon. Some volcanoes are very civilized about their eruptions. They swell up and then send out their rivers of highly liquid lava, which everyone avoids without the least difficulty, though crops, of course, are lost. Few injuries result from such eruptions, the most of them due to well-nigh unbelievable carelessness and stupidity, even on worlds without planet-wide relief programs to eliminate the problems of epidemics and starvation.

She pressed her gloved fingers to her eyes. *Not all flame mountains are nearly as well mannered. Those with high-silicate, high-water magma are much more violent. They're the ones that have smothered civilizations with gas or ash or mud. Others of their kin explode with such force that they carry great parts of their substance away with them, dozens or even hundreds of cubic miles in a cataclysm that may begin and end within seconds. They send forth killing ground quakes and seismic ocean waves that annihilate populations thousands of miles from their source. Rarest and most terrible of all are those that emit nuée ardente, glowing avalanches, not of stone but of superheated gas made so heavy by suspended particles that they must cling to the ground, incinerating all in their path.*

She sighed to herself, her mind re-creating the scenarios that culminated in those disasters.

The magma was inevitably thick, too viscous to move readily or at all or to release the gas held pent within it, ever struggling to escape. Finally, some invariably did get loose, but that release served only to worsen the pressure rather than ease it. More gas and still more escaped the confining molten material, fought to rise out of its stony prison until at last not even the weight of a mountain could hold it any longer. Weak places were found and exploited, or they were created, and all that pent-up force won free, sometimes in a single awesome instant. The exact form of that escape and its severity depended upon the conditions prevalent within the individual volcano, but any one of those horrors would prove most serious to the isolated and essentially trapped population of Strombolis.

We don't even know the Dragon's that kind of mountain, she said in near despair.

Varn Tarl Sogan sighed. *I admit I do not like the idea of climbing down into that hole, but it is hardly impossible. It should not be too difficult to get a few samples from the sides of the baby cone and some of the water as well. It is fortunate we brought the bottles with us.*

No, the woman told him hastily. *That'd be courting disaster for too little potential return. I think I may have a better idea.*

I am more than willing to consider it, he replied, smiling faintly.

According to what Bethe and Jake have found out, Strombolis' harbor is unique. Most of the island's bordered by high cliffs, many of them pierced with shallow caves at or below sea level. The better part of these are on the other side of the island, though one is quite close to the port.

So?

Those cliffs or the cave walls might show us how and of what the land was made, and they might carry signs of presettlement eruptions. By exploring them, we could pick up a few clues about the kind of Dragon with which we must deal.

We will need a boat.

Several of the port hands should have them. I'm almost certain Yeoman Lland will. No Lirman would leave all this water unexplored.

ELEVEN

VARN TARL SOGAN'S eyes rested on the sea as he paused just beyond its edge. Its clear, brilliant waters were about the sole remnant left of the Tambora that had greeted them only a few days ago. He breathed deeply of the air wafting in over its expanse. That, too, was clean, a far cry from the increasingly vile stuff that the Dragon kept spitting out.

He glanced swiftly at Bandit, who was riding his shoulder in great contentment, apparently as glad to be away from the flame mountain's emissions as he was himself. How much of it could she actually stand? Sulfur and ash only made unpleasant breathing for humans in their present concentration, but it stood to reason that they might challenge a being of the gurry's size far more heavily, especially with her spending so much time at the High Monastery, far above Strombolis proper. How much of the potentially deadly substances could she tolerate before they began to harm her for a fact?

"Be very careful up there, Bandit."

Bandit's always careful! She snuggled happily against his cheek. *Bandit misses Varn and Islaen!*

"We miss having you around, too, small one."

The man started walking again only to come to a stop once more a few seconds later, this time in response to shouts and equally loud laughter.

He had just begun to round a cluster of large, freestanding boulders that turned the center of the spaceport's section of the beach into a pretty, nicely screened little cove. He had been unable to see anything of it before now, and between the perpetual soft lapping of the water and the higher soughing of

the wind and his own preoccupation, he had been totally
unaware that it was occupied.

The crew of the *Rounder* seemed to fill the miniature beach.
Two were drying their incredibly hairy bodies on the warm
sand; the other pair were still splashing around obviously with
great pleasure in the shallow water edging the sand. Neither
ventured any farther out. Malki possessed no comparable
expanse of water, and it was unlikely that any of the four could
swim. Almost certainly, none of them could swim well.

The former Admiral shuddered in his heart. Even without his
revulsion for mutants to color his impressions, these had to be
among the ugliest beings ever to bear the title of human. In
point of fact, they were terrifying . . .

Nooo! Bandit protested with real distress. *Malkites nice!
They buy cake for Bandit!*

"You little rogue!" he whispered, laughing. "Have you been
cadging treats all over the spaceport?"

Bandit must make friends for the unit! she replied serenely.

He shook his head, but a shadow crossed his mind as he
began to stroke her. "Never board someone's ship or go into a
confined space with anyone without letting us know where you
are."

No one would hurt Bandit!

"No, but there are those who might either covet you
themselves or see you as a good sale as an exotic pet in the
inner-systems. Some renegade might try to seize you, not
realizing how much more you are or caring how your loss
would break our hearts." He had to school himself not to
hesitate on that last, for he did not speak easily of such matters
save with Islaen Connor. It was necessary that he do so here.
Bandit had only a dim grasp of monetary considerations, but
she was marvelously attuned to anything concerning the
emotions or affection.

Bandit will be careful, Varn! she promised and rubbed her
face against his.

The Arcturian sighed then. He had wanted to withdraw at
that point, but one of the Malkites had spotted him and was
waving for him to join them. Not only had Zubin fulfilled his
promise to cause no trouble, he and his mates had exerted
themselves to calm and reassure the other spacers to very good

effect. He could not be so discourteous as to turn away from their invitation now.

Suddenly Bandit sprang into the air in stark terror.

Renegade!

There was a simultaneous flash of movement from among the rocks beside him. Varn went down, flinging himself forward and to the left, but even as he moved, a blaster discharged.

He was a dead man! No one could miss at that range . . .

The gurry had not fled in her fright. She dove at the barrel of the assailant's weapon, jerking it just enough aside that the deadly bolt bypassed its intended target.

Searing agony and an even more terrible silence tore Varn Tarl Sogan's mind as he crashed into the assassin's body with measured force. The officers of the Arcturian Empire were schooled in the arts of unarmed combat, and it required only that single blow to shatter the fight in his gray-clad opponent.

He would not have stopped at that—there was a great deal of punishment a man could inflict on another without actually killing him, and he was minded to administer the full of it for this coward's work—but suddenly his opponent was gone. He had quite literally been swept out of his reach.

Sogan looked up in astonishment that would have been comical under other circumstances.

Zubin was there. He had caught the unresisting Tamboran by the arms and lifted him as if he weighed no more than a comfortably filled pack. Even as Varn watched, he gave one quick, sharp jerk and cast his victim back onto the sand where he lay alternately retching and sobbing, his shoulders so badly dislocated that they all but met behind him.

The war prince's own weapon was in his hand. "Get down, Zubin!" he hissed. "There may be more of the vermin!"

The remainder of the Malkite crew had witnessed the attack as well and had sized up the situation as readily as had their leader. They might not be Commandos, but they were no strangers to danger, natural or human-spawned. The ports they frequented were rough, and they had learned well how to take care of themselves and others of their kind in the seemingly endless war against those who sought to prey on them. None were armed, and so they kept low, making full use of the shelter provided by the great boulders comprising the formation, but it took them only a few minutes to search the whole of it thoroughly.

"No more of the port rats," one declared.

"Lucky for them," Zubin growled.

The big man came to his feet and gave his hand to Sogan. "You in one piece, Captain?"

"Sound out."

Varn barely saw him as his eyes frantically combed the sand and rock around them.

There! In one spring, he reached the limp, absolutely still gurry.

His eyes shut. No, she was not quite still. The tiny chest still rose and fell.

Gently, he scooped her up. There was no left wing. She must have taken the full bolt through it. That was what had saved her. The terrible energy had cauterized the wound, preventing her from bleeding to death.

Quickly his mind reached out and joined with Islaen's. The woman, too, had felt the little hen's anguish and her loss of consciousness, but the discipline the pair had imposed on themselves almost from their first discovery of the talent they shared had held. She had not attempted to contact him lest she distract him in battle with disastrous result. He quickly filled her in on the details of the attack and his own summary of Bandit's condition, which he knew she would confirm or correct with her own gift.

You've read it right, she assured him in the next moment, *but get her up here as soon as you can. She's going into shock.*

"The poor, brave little mote!"

He turned. Zubin sounded close to tears. His own hand shook slightly, but he kept his voice steady. "The renewer we have will soon restore her, praise the Spirit ruling space, if we can get her under treatment before shock finishes her. —Your rover? I walked down here . . ."

"It's yours, friend. Tubal'll have her back at your ship in light-speed time."

Even as he spoke, a second Malkite took the gurry from him and ran for his machine.

"Thanks, Captain Zubin. We owe you."

"Naw. This part of it's for the little mote. Anyone'd do that.

The rest . . ." He shrugged. "No one likes port rats much. It does my heart good to give one of them a shaking up."

As if to emphasize his words, he jerked their prisoner to his feet. "A Gray Robe yet! I always thought back-alley work fitted their character real well. —What do you want done with him?"

The Tamboran took one look at his intended victim's frigid, dark eyes and felt hope die within him. He was afraid of the hideous, huge man who held him and had hurt him so badly, but this one . . . He felt with a certainty that chilled his very soul that he was something scarcely human, less than human, to this guerrilla officer and that his death would be of less consequence to him than would the crushing of some biting insect.

The war prince appeared to read his terror, for his contempt became even more pronounced. "It must be kept alive for questioning," he replied indifferently. "Have your men drag it back up to the infirmary for repair. I will make formal charges and have your statements recorded there."

"Aye, Captain."

Sogan winced as the two remaining crewmen hastened to comply. His voice dropped. "Do not obey me too literally, Zubin! He is in pain enough already."

"The back-burning son of a Scythian ape deserves more than that."

"Aye, but I have never had much stomach for torture, even when it comes to vermin like this."

"Good enough. —Easy with him, lads!" he called out. "Don't kill the little rat before the brass can turn the screws on him!"

The four off-worlders started back to the port, the crewmen keeping firm hold on their whimpering prisoner.

Varn and Zubin fell into step behind them to better watch against more trouble, although neither expected anything of that nature from the severely injured Tamboran himself. There was always the chance that he might have friends.

They had traveled some minutes in silence when Sogan felt the other's gaze on him and turned to find sharp eyes studying him.

"Aye, friend?"

"You know," the Malkite said conversationally, "I've got a

face that can make one of you little chaps drop the contents of his tubes—I've known it to happen—but back there, you sounded like something out of those tapes they'd show to let us know what'd happen if the Arcturians took over."

"Unfortunately, those tapes were not entirely inaccurate," the former Admiral told him grimly. Malki's race would have been slated for immediate extermination. Even the most moderate elements would not have attempted to prevent their annihilation.

He shrugged off the chill that realization sent through him. "It is not a pleasant role, but I play it well enough for it to be useful at times."

The other nodded and grinned. "It was a real knock to that misbegotten little planet hugger, right enough. He probably thought we'd treat him like some kind of martyr. —It's the galactic pen for him, I suppose?"

"That more or less depends on the results of his testing, but I would feel safe in putting down credits that he will not be out roaming the streets of Strombolis for a long time to come."

Tubal did not spare his rover in getting his tiny charge to the *Fairest Maid*. It remained parked by the boarding ramp for several minutes, then rumbled back toward the beach at a saner pace. Mind and eyes told Sogan that it carried a passenger. Two passengers. Islaen and a fully restored and very excited gurry.

Bandit did not wait for the vehicle to reach them before spinning from it and literally flinging herself upon Varn. Her sharp claws dug into the collar of his tunic as her wings extended to the full in an attempt to encircle his throat.

"Now, small one, you were wounded, not I," he told her softly aloud and, with far greater feeling, in mind. His pleasure at seeing her whole again was such that he felt no embarrassment at her display of affection, nor did it seem to him that he was lessened by it in the eyes of any of those watching despite their broad, sharp-toothed grins.

"She's fine now," the woman assured them all. "What about you, Varnt? Are you sure . . ."

"There is nothing wrong with me apart from having half a pound of beach sand ground into my clothes and skin."

Zubin clapped him on the shoulder. "He could just use a

good, stiff drink, Colonel. We'll stand him to that once we unload this cargo of space slime."

Varn, please . . .

I know, Colonel, he replied with a mental grimace. Their appearance aside, he liked the rough Malkites, especially after seeing the feeling they had shown for the injured gurry, but the promised drink was another matter. Apart from an occasional glass of fine wine, officers of the Empire did not use alcohol, and the Federation's most highly prized potions tasted villainous to him, much less the quick-processed concoctions he could expect to find in a backwater hole like this.

Islaen only laughed. *Enjoy yourself, Admiral. Don't come home drunk to me.*

I should do that to teach you a lesson! he grumbled as he raised his hand in a gesture of farewell.

"You had no warning at all until he attacked?" Jake Karmikel asked the Arcturian when he returned to the *Fairest Maid.*

Sogan shook his head. "None." He sat in his customary place. "All was peaceful, and then he was on us."

"We can assume the attack wasn't premeditated at that rate," the Commando-Colonel told her comrades. "Varn wouldn't have been able to pick up his transmissions, but Bandit sure as space would've."

Bandit knew he was there! He was just looking at the Malkites!

"All right, small one. You are not to blame."

Varn translated what she had said for Bethe and Jake.

Islaen's brows drew together. "The way I see it, he must have crept down for a look-see, and something just set him off."

"My race?" Varn Tarl Sogan suggested wearily. It was an old pattern . . .

To his surprise, the woman shook her head. "I doubt it. Most of us in any way close to prototype probably look rather alike to Tamborans, even those who've been off-world. Beyond that, they never really hated Arcturians all that much, not any more than they do any other race not their own. I'd say it was more likely your Commando uniform. That epitomizes the military and everything else they do detest. Or he could simply have snapped at that moment."

"You both think he was acting on his own?" Bethe asked.

"Aye," Varn responded. "Just about certainly. The Abbot would not risk revealing the fact that there were armed Tamborans, not yet, even if he were sending down spies. He would most assuredly not do so before off-worlders."

"The blaster?"

"Service issue. His own. Islaen had a check on the serial done first thing."

"What about your prisoner himself?" Jake asked. "Any idea when we can expect to get a crack at him?"

"Not for a while," Islaen told him. "Physician's orders. His heart is apparently not overly sound, and our friend Zubin did a proper job on him. Any more shocks, and there could be no one to grill at all." She sighed. "It could be worse. We don't expect to get much from him anyway."

"You sent the locals a report, I suppose?"

She nodded indifferently. "To the Commissar. There's been no response, of course, but they do have a right to know that one of their own's up to his windpipe in trouble."

The surplanetary transceiver buzzed. The Colonel excused herself and spoke into it for a couple of seconds, then turned back to the others. "It looks like we wronged our hosts. That was Yeoman Lland from the gate. We are about to have a visitor."

"A lawyer?" Jake inquired in surprise. "I didn't even think they'd have any."

"Commissar Strombol himself."

Bethe's brows raised. "I guess Jake and I had better vanish. He won't want to talk before too large an audience."

"That might be best," the other woman agreed. "He has to be in some state to come to us at all."

"We'll wait on the bridge."

"Good enough. —Varn, stay with me, and Bandit. You both are the injured parties in all this."

Ivan Strombol clambered up the boarding ramp. His small eyes shifted uneasily as he passed through the air lock, but otherwise, he held his nervousness and distaste in good check as he exchanged greetings with the Commandos and allowed them to escort him aboard their vessel.

Once they were within the crew's cabin, he turned and faced them. There was an ashen hue to his complexion, and even before he spoke, both were fully aware of the shock the incident had been for him. The man was a genuine pacifist, and his horror of the violence so nearly perpetrated by one of his kind was real and very sharp.

"Colonel Connor, Captain Sogan, I came as soon as my duties permitted to offer ye my deepest apologies both in Tambora's name and in my own. I realize the words sound empty and how empty they would be in fact had that renegade succeeded, but they are heartfelt." He shuddered. "I still cannot believe that such an incident could have occurred here and at the hand of one of my own people."

"Tambora's not to blame, sir. It was one person's deed, and we're nearly certain that he probably can't be held responsible for it."

"The boy, what will ye do to him? I understand he was injured in the capture."

The Noreenan frowned slightly. "Man, sir. He's at least one age to Varnt. —To answer your last question first, his shoulders have been reset, and he's resting comfortably in the infirmary under strict watch by the medical staff. You will have a complete report on his condition in the morning. Sooner if you require it.

"As for his future, he must face Federation justice. His crime was against service personnel."

"We do not deny that," the Commissar sighed. "Tambora will make no protest."

"Thank you, sir. Again, you'll be kept fully informed about every aspect of the case. Unfortunately, Tambora has no solicitors trained in military law, but you may have observers present to assure that his interests are not violated, though any protest must be made through appropriate channels. No disruption of the justice process will be permitted."

"That is understood as well."

"The prisoner will have to be evaluated. Should he prove to be insane, as we believe is most likely, he'll be humanely confined in a facility designed to house those like himself. If he is competent to stand trial, it will be before a military tribunal."

"The trial, it will be just?"

"Aye. The Navy runs a tight, hard court, but they do go for the truth."

Ivan paused. "That accursed weapon. Where did he get that? Who would have sold it to him?"

That was the first touch of hostility the Tamboran had shown, and Sogan hastened to answer him. "No one, sir. It was his own. Service issue. He had to have brought it back with him."

"You are certain of that?"

"We are, sir. The serial confirms it, and there is no record of its having been returned to the Navy or sold."

"Why?" Strombol asked. "Why should any son of this peaceful world want to keep possession of such a-thing?"

Islaen Connor watched him with real pity. The question and anguish on him were painful to receive.

"Sit down, Commissar Strombol," she told him. "There could be one very good reason, and if I'm right about that, there could be a hell of a lot more blasters holed up on Tambora of Pele waiting to fulfill no good purpose."

In as few words as possible, the Commando-Colonel outlined the threat his government might be facing.

Strombol's expression darkened as she continued, and he would have exploded as soon as she fell silent had she not cut him off with a sharp wave of her hand. "Think, man! It's a small thing, but you did inform the Abbot of this incident, didn't you?"

"Of course. The man is part of his community, or was," he responded frigidly.

"You came to us, because you are a human being shocked by his deed and because you are Tambora's representative. You thought to inquire about this erring citizen's fate. Why have we heard nothing at all from the man to whom he reported?"

"We are a restrained, well-ordered people," Ivan insisted stubbornly. "Nothing like this . . ."

"Rot!" she snapped. "What about your own illustrious ancestor?"

Varn Tarl Sogan had been watching Islaen in some surprise, masking most of his thoughts behind carefully raised shields, but now he entered the argument. "That first Commissar worked his change of government without hate and without the use of weapons, but these are different times. Tamboran may not hate Tamboran, though we have no proof of that, but there is strong, long-fostered resentment against the off-worlders living and working here, and there may be weapons such as that which the assassin tried to use on me. It would not require many to create a bloodbath on a world where there is little or nothing to resist them."

"That would be a complete violation of my people's basic nature!" the other man gasped in horror.

"Perhaps, sir, but you were originally seed of Terra. I grant that the Gray Abbot may not realize what he may be doing, not fully, since he has had no more experience with the potential result than anyone else on this planet, but if he works his people up to such an emotional state that they are willing to revolt against your authority for him, to handle the weapons they hate for his sake, that very emotion may sweep some of them. You saw an example of what can happen. That was but one man, as well. A mob is something else, basically mindless and ever ready to fling off all control and direction."

Ivan eyed him, stung to the soul by what he saw as an open slur on all his race, yet impressed despite himself. The alien pair might be dead wrong—they must be—but they believed fully in the reality of the peril they described.

Unfortunately, so must he. He was Tambora's Commissar, and the welfare of his planet and his people rested on him. He could not ignore such a threat, however impossible everything within him declared it to be.

"What do you suggest I do, Captain? Search the Gray monasteries for blasters?"

"If you acted quickly and in force and were then prepared to seize the arms and banish those possessing or having knowledge of them, you should be able to abort the rebellion, assuming you were open in giving the truth to your people."

The Noreenan touched Strombol's shoulder gently. "There are never easy answers in a situation like this, sir, but you are Tambora's leader. We had to make you aware of our suspicions. How you act on them, that must be your decision, and you may well believe that neither of us envies you the making of it."

TWELVE

THE GRAY ROBE'S attack and the formalities that had followed it cost the pair the remainder of that day, and it was late the following morning before they were able to pick up their plan to explore the cliffs and caves facing the island.

They saw as soon as they looked up at the fire mountain that the Dragon had shown them a great deal of consideration the previous day. Beginning late in the evening and continuing all through the night and early morning, it had spewed forth an almost constant stream of ash and fumes, and its inner working so increased in strength that its rumblings were now clearly audible in both port and city.

The sky all about the summit had filled in and darkened, partly with steam and ash, partly with thunder clouds. The volume of water being dumped upon it was clearly illustrated by the vast swelling of the usually tiny streams cascading down its sides, although no rain at all fell upon the inhabited regions below.

Sogan watched the ever-thickening screen with no little awe. They had made their ascent none too soon. There would be no going up through that and maybe none after it cleared once more, either, if it did stop. He remembered the steepness of some of those slopes and the difficulty the ash that had already fallen had given them. That much again would have come down during the last several hours, maybe enough to render the peak totally inaccessible. A very little more certainly would do so.

His mind touched Islaen's in greeting as she joined him on the *Maid*'s bridge.

She gave one glance at the glowering mountain and made a quick prayer of gratitude to Tambora's gods that they would not have to face its slopes today, then turned resolutely to the man. *Ready for a sail?*

If you found a boat for us.

Issicar Lland's. He has one, just as I thought. He's fond of her, too, she added mischievously. *I couldn't decide whether his doubts about this excursion stemmed more from concern for her safety than fear for ours.*

The Arcturian smiled. *I can hardly blame him. Commandos are known to be hard on equipment at times.*

His mood sobered. *Why did you tell Strombol about our suspicions yesterday? Do you now believe our work lies more with the volcano than with the potential rebellion?*

She thought for a few moments before answering him. *Perhaps in a sense,* she conceded. *That madman or whatever he is gave us the opening by revealing the possession of weapons by native Tamborans, and there really is little we can do, or maybe should do, as long as the Alpha Gary arms aren't involved.*

The Dragon is Tamboran business as well, he pointed out.

Aye, but it is so deadly, and they all seem so blind to it . . .

I know, my Islaen, the former Admiral told her softly. *We cannot just let that go.*

Both were quiet for several seconds. At last, Sogan turned away from the gripping, dark spectacle of the mountain. *I have not seen our comrades this morning.*

Bandit's up at the High Monastery again. The newlyweds are locked aboard the Moon *waiting to hear from Horus. I've asked for a full report on what happened to the blasters issued to the Tamboran troops, not just general assurances. Any we can't account for as returned or sold, we can pretty safely assume are somewhere on-world. It'll be something to give the Commissar anyway.* She laughed softly. *They were happy to be relieved of their research assignment. Our hosts apparently don't deal in very stirring prose.*

The two guerrillas were not long in walking down to the water despite the heavy covering of ash and readily found the dock where the Lirman's craft was tied.

She was a little vessel, Varn saw, small and slender and obviously of extremely light weight, perfect for one man's handling. She was powered by either sail or oars or by both; the offspring of Lir did not admit machines to their pleasure craft, counting such as the grim slaves of commerce and a screen between them and their beloved oceans.

Her name was the *Daber,* one common to the maids of Lir.

Well, Admiral, do you think you can manage her? his consort teased.

Varn Tarl Sogan had taken to water as quickly and naturally as he had years earlier taken to space itself, and he was already the master of any of his comrades in that element.

That, we shall soon find out, Colonel Connor.

The sea was smooth and fair, the wind strong enough to move the *Daber* swiftly over its bright surface but not to give argument for control of the vessel.

The Arcturian kept her well in, enough away from the cliff so as not to risk snagging her on some submerged rock but near enough to have a good look at the stone comprising it.

When they approached the first sea cave, he deftly lowered the sails and maneuvered inside with the oars.

For a moment, all was shrouded in a pleasantly warm twilight until they switched on the powerful raditorches they had brought to aid their explorations.

The cave was small, only twenty-odd square feet, but its walls had much to tell, and it was a sober pair who left it again to continue their journey around the Dragon's island.

The sailing remained almost uniformly easy. There was no change in the strength of the water's flow, no perceptible tides or currents to trouble them. Only when they passed near those places where the swollen streams drained into the ocean did they encounter turbulence, but then it was of sufficient power to test Sogan's skill with the light vessel, and he tried to give them fairly wide berth.

He had no difficulty in sighting them. Such spots were an unsightly stain on the normally brilliant sea, dark with brown soil and gray ash and with mats of vegetation, even good-sized branches, broken off by the constantly increasing weight of the Dragon's ejecta.

Islaen Connor studied this debris grimly, sadly, whenever

they passed near some stream's discharge. That ugly sludge represented the ruin of much that had been beautiful.

She straightened suddenly as they were about to cross the last of the river mouths. *Go in closer, Varn.*

The man obeyed, fighting to hold his boat steady until the Colonel bent over the side to scoop up whatever had caught her eye. After that, he took the *Daber* out to quieter water once more.

What have you found? he asked curiously as she continued to study her discovery intently.

In answer, she held up a limp little bundle of ash-caked feathers so tiny that it barely covered her small hand.

Islaen caressed the pathetic corpse with her left forefinger. *If I'm right, and it died of asphyxiation, then the Dragon has already proven itself not only a death threat but a source of death for at least some of Tambora's denizens.*

The Commandos returned the *Daber* to her moorings with a heavy heart and reported their findings to their comrades.

They had accomplished a great deal in the time they had been out. Of chief importance, they had succeeded in observing the heartstone of Strombolis' island. It was volcanic, as was inevitable, and of a type formed from very high-silica magma. Whether its water content had also been high, that they had not been able to determine by visual observation even with the detailed information the volcanologists had supplied, but given everything else, that, too, was at least very likely.

Once the spaceport forensic medic confirmed that the little bird had indeed died of asphyxiation, Islaen Connor went to the bridge. She remained there a long time, and when she did return to her companions, she was as grim as they had ever seen her.

She sat down, her head lowered, oblivious to the steaming jakek the Sergeant pushed toward her.

"Our scientists think we could be in big trouble," the Colonel told them without attempting to soften her concern. "General consensus is that the Dragon's certain to go, and when it does, it's likely to do it fast and violently. What no one will venture to guess at this point is precisely what it will do and how long we have before it blows.

"The Navy's coming with an evacuation fleet and a full

scientific team, but it'll take several days to get here, and they say we simply may not have anything like that much time. We'll just have to shift for ourselves until they can reach us."

"How?" demanded the Noreenan man angrily. "It's not a bloody wolf pack we're facing here!"

Her expression hardened. "Right now, I'm going to see Commissar Strombol." She glanced at her consort. "I'll need you with me, Varn. For moral support if nothing else." Her voice trembled slightly. "I may be about to take command of this whole damned planet."

THIRTEEN

ONCE MORE, VARN Tarl Sogan found himself in dress uniform en route to the Commissar's palace. This time, though, he and the Commando-Colonel rode in the rear of the flier while Jake Karmikel acted the part of chauffeur. Every formality had to be observed in a mission of this urgency.

It was the first time he had been given any peace since their return from their tour of the island, and he rested his head against the seat as he sent his mind out in search of their Jadite comrade.

Bandit, are you all right? He could not rid himself of the image of the dead bird his consort had fished out of the sea. It had been no bigger than the gurry, and it was too easy to imagine her coughing out her life as that pitiful little creature must have done.

The answer came without delay. *Yes, Varn! Bandit's being careful!*

The mountain is worse, small one. It has started killing things higher up. Come back at once.

Soon!—Important here, Varn! Right now! Bandit can't describe! Link!

Islaen's mind had been joined with his. She straightened beside him. "Do what she wants," she told him, aloud to let Jake know what was happening. "She's never given us a false lead yet."

Go ahead, small one. I am ready.

Sogan closed his eyes to cut down on the contradictory impressions pouring into his mind as his sense receptors suddenly joined with the hen's. There was an instant of wrenching disorientation, then his vision cleared.

103

He found himself looking down upon a large stone room bare of furnishings except for a wooden lectern in its center. A gray-clad man whose robe was edged in orange stood before this, while a large number of others knelt around him.

The Arcturian's heart felt cold. They were holding blasters, some aloft, some outstretched, some merely resting on their laps. All had their eyes closed as they concentrated on the weapons and on the words of their leader.

The Abbot, for so the orange stripe on his clothing proclaimed him to be, was telling them to consider the tools of evil they held, that they were tools, no more than that, tools that could be used to cleanse evil as well as perform it, cleanse it from their own people . . .

So, he hissed as his sight and hearing returned to their normal seat. Quickly he described what he had seen for Karmikel's sake. The Colonel had remained linked with him and had shared his observations directly.

"It's about what we thought," the redhead said.

"He hopes to move soon and is pushing his believers," Islaen mused. "They're not anywhere like ready yet. The Dragon must be spooking him, or all of them, too."

"How long do we have?" Sogan asked her.

"Who knows? They're listening, but from what I could feel, there's no fire in any of them."

Jake shook his head. "You'll have to clean that lot out and fast if you have to seize the planet, Islaen. That'd give them the push they need if anything will."

"I know," she replied grimly. Her career would probably be finished if she did. Taking temporary control to combat the menace of the fire mountain was one matter. Taking military action against a respected and ancient surplanetary institution and seizing the legal personal property of the inhabitants for political reasons, before any attack had been made on her party, would not be so readily accepted; it formed too deadly a precedent for that.

"Cheer up, Colonel," her fellow Noreenan told her. "There's always the Dragon. That could still put an end to all such problems for us.—You told Bandit to come back down, Admiral?"

"She is on her way. I ordered her to return to the *Maid* and to wait there with Bethe. I did not want her trying to locate us in all this ash."

None of the three spoke again during the remainder of the journey. The gravity of the Colonel's errand, the implication of it for all of them, weighed too heavily on them.

The world around their closed vehicle was deathly still. The heavy layer of ash now on the ground kept pedestrians off the streets. People hesitated to so much as open a door or window unnecessarily, for to do so was to admit the clinging stuff to shop or home.

This present downfall was constant and heavy enough that had their vehicle been equipped with conventional wipers, they would have been forced to stop to clear the windshield off manually several times already. Luckily, Jake had amused himself one morning by installing a blower system when the ashfalls began to become a regular feature of life on Tambora, and that kept the viewing surface clean for them.

Twilight was well advanced by the time the Commando vehicle drew to a halt before Strombol's dwelling.

Karmikel opened the door for his two passengers, then went back inside the flier to await their return. Ostensibly, he was sitting at close attention, but in fact, he was watching the pair intently lest they be given trouble in effecting an entrance.

His fine features were frozen in a hard, determined mask. He was not about to permit Islaen Connor to be harried at this stage, not with the weight of Strombolis' life resting on her.

Islaen herself was wondering what sort of reception they would receive, although she gave no sign of any uncertainty in her manner. She knew she could afford no display of weakness now, when it was total control of the planet that she must have if she could gain her will by no lesser means.

As on their previous visit, there were two porters at the door. From the looks they bent on the off-worlders and their manner, it was patent that they would have preferred barring the way, but custom forbade the denying of the palace to anyone seeking entrance there, and they grudgingly stood aside.

Once within, they were soon confronted by the same woman who had served as their guide earlier.

She was not chained by tradition as were her fellows outside, and she so firmly stood her ground before them that the two newcomers were forced to come to a halt. "The Commissar is a busy man. He is at his dinner now, but he keeps the usual hours tomorrow. If ye wish another interview with him, ye may make your petitions properly then."

Varn Tarl Sogan's voice cut into her like the lash of a force whip. "We have come on behalf of the Federation Senate under such conditions as will brook no delay. Inform Commissar Strombol that Colonel Connor and I will see him at once."

The Tamboran stared at him. The authority on the man was unmistakable, as was the fact that he was determined to have his will by whatever means he felt compelled to use in order to gain it. She hesitated only an instant before turning and hastening out of their presence.

Sogan's hand closed over Islaen's. *Strombol hated us for our suspicions against his Gray Robes, but he proved himself enough his people's leader to listen. He may do so again now and not force you to take over command of Tambora. It is not necessary that we like one another to work together to save Strombolis.*

No, of course not. She sighed. *I hope you're right, Varn, but the Dragon is such an emotional issue with these Tamborans. I don't know what it'll actually take to wake him up.*

The threat of losing control to a pack of hated aliens might. Cooperating with us would at least allow him to keep his hands on the drive.

It'll be easier all around if he does. People in trouble respond best to their own.

They drew apart again as Islaen felt the angry pattern of the returning Tamboran woman.

"This way," she commanded them sourly.

They followed her down a different set of corridors from those leading to the office. This time, she led them to a much smaller and more warmly furnished chamber, an eating room in which a meal had obviously been in progress moments before, although the table was now cleared of food and only one individual remained within.

Ivan Strombol barely chained his fury enough to speak coherently. "What is the meaning of this intrusion?"

"I am sorry for it, Commissar," Islaen Connor replied coldly, "but a volcano does not necessarily keep to Federation-standard hours."

The other responded with a vicious oath. "I have already told ye the Dragon is harmless."

"I disagree, Commissar. Its past gives testimony to life, not extinction, and already it has well exceeded historical precedent.

"It has been ejecting both ash and lapilli in increasing volume and frequency. It emits steam and gas and has produced a sizable hot lake in its crater. It has generated some ground tremors, and its roaring has been constantly audible for over twelve hours now. It has set fur snakes and other wildlife moving down from the upper slopes and has begun to kill off flora and even fauna.—We were at the summit, Commissar, and we've examined a little of the structure of this island. The judgment I have just received from our volcanologists only confirms my own conclusion that your mountain is going to blow and blow very soon."

"You dared," Ivan hissed, "dared to draw still other off-worlders into Tamboran business?"

"As senior officer in Pele's system, I was without choice. Federation citizens were threatened, and local authorities were making no move to assure their safety. It was necessary for me to take action."

"Did it ever occur to you that perhaps those local authorities know . . ." he began.

Sogan brought his fist down sharply on the table. "You self-blinded fools know nothing! Not only have you refused every request to investigate conditions here, but you have labeled most learning as an evil to be avoided and so have failed to train your own people to study your planet. In the face of her history, that is not mere stupidity; it is gross negligence."

"Her history is one of total peace. Never in all the centuries since Tambora's discovery has there been the slightest significant natural disturbance."

"Centuries? They mean something in a colony's life, perhaps, but they are no more than motes in geological time. Tambora of Pele was once incredibly active, and until it is unequivocally proven that similar violence is impossible now, the potential for her becoming so once again must be presumed."

All right, Varn. Let up on him.

Islaen forced herself to speak reasonably. "Look, I know you don't like to take more on yourself than the daily duties tradition lays on you, but the call to go beyond that in time of need is inherent in the place you hold. Your own ancestor, that first Commissar Strombol, acted decisively when it became evident the Orange Ascetics would bring the colony to total destruction in very short order. Since then, fate has been kind, and his descendants have ruled a paradise where their greatest concern has been to keep their people away from strangers lest curiosity about the stars and those who roam between them be thereby aroused."

She quickly moved away from that emotionally dangerous topic. "Fortune hasn't been so sparing of you. Tambora herself has risen up to challenge you, and you can't, you don't dare, ignore her."

"If I do, you think to seize control of Tambora yourself?" Strombol demanded bitterly.

"I've already been authorized to do so, but why should it be necessary?—Man, these are your own people! Do you want them dead?"

"There is no danger. Even should I be wrong about the Dragon, it is over four miles away from the city, and the island is a large one."

"With some few people on every part of it," she pointed out.

The Noreenan shook her head. "Mountains of the Dragon's type have been known to blow a third of their substance into the air and drop the bulk of the fragments straight down on some local community, that or shatter islands larger than this one into pebbles and then drown what's left in a series of massive waves."

Ivan never made reply. A deafeningly loud, sharp clap silenced him. A deeper, infinitely fiercer roar followed fast upon it.

Instinctively, he whirled about and raced for that part of the terrace circling the upper story of the palace that faced upon the mountain. The two intruders came after him.

The sky was now nearly black, but a great cloud of deeper blackness rolled high and wide above the Dragon. Lightning flashed through it, streaks, arcs, indescribable pinwheel forms, sheets that purpled vast billows, throwing them into momentary eldritch relief against the whole terrible thing.

Varn's consciousness of himself returned suddenly. He found he had moved very close to Islaen. His arm was around her, his body between her and the fire mountain. She cringed full against him but was looking up, directly into what might well be their doom.

He drew a deep, slow breath as the cloud continued to rise. It spread out, thinning as it passed far overhead, showering Strombolis with pebbles and large stones as it went.

Very quietly, Sogan released the woman. She turned to Ivan Strombol. "I refuse to believe that thirty thousand utter fools inhabit this city. Those people out there have to be afraid, and if nothing is done to relieve that fear, if no concrete move is made in their defense, they will panic. That's a contagious disease, Commissar. Only a very few can start a dance of death such as perhaps even the mountain will not bring should its assault be gentler than I suppose."

The Commissar stared into the now-peaceful blackness. His body was stiff with fury, and it was a full two minutes and better before he could bring himself to speak. "Very well, Colonel. What so-called cooperation do you demand?"

"Calm, quick compliance with the evacuation order when the fleet arrives . . ."

"You cannot be serious!"

"What else can be done with your people until the island can be declared safe once more? Volcanologists are coming with our ships and hopefully will be able to arrive at a speedy answer as to how long that will be."

She pressed on swiftly before the other regained the will for argument. "Since we cannot be sure the Navy can reach us in time, I want everything on Tambora that floats brought into this vicinity, close enough to start removing the entire population and bearing them over the horizon within one hour of my command to do so."

"That would take every vessel on the planet," the other protested in dismay, "and most cannot reach us any sooner than your Navy."

Islaen did not challenge that. It only confirmed what she herself had feared. "Summon them all. We'll have to use what we can in the time available, probably bringing the populace away in stages, the sick and the young going first . . ."

"Separating families," Ivan rumbled darkly.

"With an island community on so low-tech a planet, we don't have a whole lot of choice. Your little ones must be given the first and best chance for survival."

She raised her hands, forestalling the other's refired anger. "Sorry, Commissar. I mean Tambora of Pele no insult. My own homeworld is also low-tech, and I well appreciate the advantages of maintaining a world as you have done, but there are disadvantages as well, and those are working against us now. We have to do the best we can with the resources open to us.

"Each person is to bring two days' supply of food and water plus an equal amount for any animals you possess."

Fortunately, the native species were all small, and the settlers had never imported anything other than a few companion animals from the stars. Because there was no commercial interest in livestock, they at least would not have to concern themselves with transporting big, nonintelligent creatures. A few little household pets would not present any problems.

The Noreenan glanced up at the mountain. There were so many ways in which it could slay, some of them effective at great distance. Could she, could anyone, possibly identify and counter them all, counter those that would actually come into play here?

"Warning must also be sent to each of the other islands so that their inhabitants will be prepared to move to high ground, a minimum of two hundred feet above the sea, again within an hour's notice."

"Two hundred feet!" Strombol gasped.

The thought of the force of water necessitating such a flight seemed to stun him more than any of Islaen's descriptions of the volcano's other potential hazards.

The Colonel nodded. "That is probably well overdoing it," she conceded, "but I don't dare cut it finer, not knowing the history of waves in other places—This, at least, shouldn't be a completely strange trouble to you. High water in the storm season must have forced upward evacuation many times in one place or another over the years."

It was a quick guess but an accurate one, she saw, as the other lowered his head in assent. "Aye. That is why we have been compelled to maintain planet-wide aural communication.

Wind waves rise quickly and travel far on our ocean, and there can be no delay in transmitting warning of their approach."

"That's a mercy now, at any rate."

Strombol looked as if he heartily disagreed, but he did not challenge the Commando. "What about your people?" he asked instead.

"I can't answer for any of the spacers, of course, but the port personnel and the Patrol unit will evacuate with Strombolis."

A sudden fire flickered for a moment in her eyes as the lightning had torn through the Dragon's cloud minutes before. "I'll grant them this much. I won't sacrifice any of them for you Tamborans once the children are away. They'll get equal and perhaps first priority in the boats.

"So that is your service's vaunted impartiality!" the Commissar jeered.

Islaen merely shrugged. "Most of them are civilians, and even were they not, I should still give the same orders concerning them. You've refused port workers the right to have fliers because you did not want strangers in your skies. You denied them the right to use boats larger than a dinghy because you didn't wish to encounter them on your sea or have them become intimate with her. As a result, you have deprived them of the means of securing their safety themselves from a peril that should have been studied and anticipated had you not prevented that work. These people have a right to claim their lives from you now."

"Then let them go at once, as the first group, before you begin to disturb Tamboran citizens."

The Arcturian gave him an ugly smile. "Four Commandos and six Patrol agents are a small number to enforce an unwelcome order even upon a people as quiet as yours, as I think you well realize, Commissar. No, the off-worlders stay with us until Colonel Connor is ready to release them."

"To be used as thugs against us?" Strombol demanded with a frown. He had not imagined before that the Colonel would go so far, but facing this Sogan, seeing the hardness and determination on him, he had his doubts. He was capable of a great deal, and so, too, was the woman, for all the deeper velvet sheathing her claws.

The Commando-Colonel answered for her consort, although her manner was fully as unbending as his. "There will be no abuse, but I do warn you to see that no temptation be given to provoke it. These people are human or the equivalent, and they resent, many of them bitterly, the treatment they've been accorded here. They might be only too glad to physically assist a Gray Robe into a boat, for instance, if he were somewhat slow in boarding."

A dark stain suffused the Tamboran's normally monochromatic features. "Are you aware that so much as a touch by an off-worlder . . ."

"Aye, and so are my people. Just see to it that we have no problems, overt or covert, during the evacuation, and you should have nothing to worry about in terms of insult."

"There will be no trouble from us, but, Colonel, enjoy your rank while you may, because once this is over, I shall see you stripped of it and of your freedom for most of all of what remains to you of life."

"It is your prerogative to try. However, while you're pondering the charges to bring against me, it might be well to recall that the attempt to block or in any manner interfere with Navy or Stellar Patrol communications is an extremely grave offense."

For an instant, rage and fear were both open upon the Commissar, but in the next moment he had regained full command over himself. "What sort of nonsense is this?"

The woman met his question with a cold laugh. "Do you think we're complete vacuum brains, Strombol? Our equipment and the personnel who use it were honed against the Arcturian Intelligence Service. We had discovered and were monitoring your station within twenty-four hours of your first attempt against us. We could have done it in less than ten minutes had we so willed."

Her head turned, and she looked steadily in the direction of the now-invisible Dragon for several seconds. After that, she faced the surplanetary leader once more.

"All this may have little actual relevance. We have a common enemy with the power to annihilate us and every other living thing on this island at any moment it chooses. I suggest we concentrate on doing what we can to prevent that from happening and leave our private divisions for a time when we have more leisure to indulge them."

Islaen Connor turned from him and, motioning Varn to

follow her, abruptly left the terrace and then the dining chamber itself.

Without waiting for their unwilling guide to appear, the guerrillas retraced the route they had traveled to reach the Commissar's apartments until they came once more to the broad doors of the palace.

FOURTEEN

JAKE ALL BUT leaped from his vehicle when the pair appeared. He was beside them in a moment. "Islaen, Admiral, are you both all right?"

"Aye, of course we are," the Arcturian replied curtly. "That was not a Thugee's lair in there."

The woman's smile softened the harshness of her companion's words. "We were in full command of the situation from the time we entered the palace," she assured him.

Karmikel opened the door for them and took his own place at the controls. "You did succeed, I suppose?" He had spent the time since they had left him in a state of deep anxiety that had been in no way lessened by the shock the volcano had given him.

"Aye," Sogan answered grimly. "The Dragon made the victory an easy one for us. Its intervention put an end to what would have been a long and very unpleasant argument."

He felt a shudder pass through Islaen and looked down at her. As he had done earlier, but this time with full consciousness, he brought his arm around her.

She was as tired and frightened as he was, he thought, and she still had a night ahead of her. There would have to be reports to Horus and to the scientists speeding toward Pele's system and to the Patrol unit back at the port. It would be well after midnight before she could so much as consider knocking out.

Whatever her weariness, there was no complaint from the Noreenan, and her fortitude made him long all the more to give her ease, ease and safety.

The woman, for her part, was content to rest against him. There was comfort in his strength and warmth, and for these few, brief moments, she felt secure even from the threat glowering over them all.

They were a long time at Patrol headquarters and longer still on the bridge of the *Fairest Maid*, for Islaen's report to Admiral Sithe was extremely detailed and involved. So, too, was that which she made immediately afterward to the volcanologists en route to the imperiled planet.

When at long last the weary pair came down to the crew's cabin, it was to face yet another interrogation, but this one was informal, relaxed. There was no weight of interstellar politics on them here, no need for ritual, no necessity to hold any pose of strength or mystery or superiority before Jake Karmikel or Bethe Danlo or the tired but ever-interested gurry.

Karmikel turned to his commander as soon as she had completed her account of the evening's events. "How did Strombol seem to you? What kind of readings did you pick up from him?"

"He hates us, more than he hates the concept of off-worlders defiling Tambora, more than he fears the volcano, more than he loves the life of his body or his soul. If duty were less ingrained in every fiber of him, I'd be really worried about him, and as it is, he'll be our implacable foe once this is ended."

"Never mind about later. Will he cooperate now?"

She nodded. "He will. He'll not play his people false. Indeed, I think he's glad of what we've done in one sense. He can take the precautions necessary to preserve his folk and set the blame for it all on us if the Dragon quiets once more. —He does believe us now, I think, though at first, when the explosion hit, his foremost reaction after the initial shock was one of suspicion and anger, as if he thought we'd set charges on the peak when we were up there, even though logic and every sense must have told him that was beyond any mere human agency."

The woman sighed. "I wonder how much of this is my fault, the result of my mishandling . . ."

"None!" snapped Varn. "You were a master during the whole of it. There was no change of thought or mood, no nuance in him, that you failed to meet and either counter or strengthen as need demanded."

"I made an enemy, Varn Tarl Sogan. That much I know."

"What of it?" he demanded. "He would never have been our friend. Had you handled it differently, he would have tried to thwart you at every turn, maybe causing enough delay to render our efforts worthless. Now you have at least his respect and, with it, his cooperation, although he will probably try to seek a heavy revenge later."

"The Dragon may do the job for him," the other man said gloomily. "That was an impressive display tonight."

"Too impressive."

Islaen Connor looked from one to the other of them. They were all frightened, right enough, and had every reason to be.

For a moment, she thought of lifting, of leaving Strombolis to its fate, or at least of sending Jake and Bethe off with the *Jovian Moon.*

They would not go.

Varn! Stay out of a person's supposedly private thoughts!

They were not shielded. Besides, you rarely check Bandit for her inability to do that.

You are not as cute as Bandit! She sighed. *I know they won't go, Varn. I don't suppose I could send you away, either, and you heartily dislike Tamborans.*

No. I stay. I may detest these people, but I cannot leave them, no more than you can, even if we accomplish nothing more in the end than lift with a handful of refugees who would otherwise perish along with the multitude we may fail to save.

His shoulders straightened. *There is no profit in this. We are both bone-weary. Let us knock out now, my Islaen, and leave the future to its own devices for a while.*

FIFTEEN

THE FORMER ADMIRAL fell asleep quickly but soon woke again to find that he could not drift off a second time.

He lay still, staring up at the dark-screened ceiling of his minute cabin.

So much seemed to be happening so quickly since their arrival on Tambora of Pele. It did not matter, or seem to matter, that they had not actually come into real danger yet. Fate was drawing a dark noose around them all. He could feel it pull tighter with every passing second . . .

Sogan tossed his head. They had a budding revolution and a volcano getting ready to erupt on their hands. That was more than enough to fill his mind without giving his imagination full rein as well. One with his training should have better control over himself than that.

He wondered how the Colonel was faring, if she was lying awake and in turmoil even as he was, and his mind reached out to her. He moved slowly, carefully, lest he disturb his consort's rest. She had been so weary and so heavily burdened when they had separated . . .

He soon found Bandit, blissfully asleep in her spider-silk nest in the Noreenan's cabin. He left her quickly, gently, so that she should not feel his seeking and be drawn back into wakefulness.

Varn sat up. Islaen was not aboard the *Fairest Maid*.

Crushing all other thought, he sent his probe out farther, beyond the confines of the starship.

He soon located her. She was on the ramp, and despair only radiated from her.

The Arcturian felt an icy knot forming in his stomach. What was the Dragon doing now? Why had the woman not called him?

He did not want to know! His courage failed him, and he desired only to bury his face in his pillow, to sink into it, to sleep away this dark terror the universe had become.

Sogan began dressing mechanically. One could not pretend an eruptive volcano did not exist. That was what the Tamborans were trying to do. Islaen had given him a half-serious chance to escape tonight, and he had freely chosen to cast it away in the only decision his humanity and manhood had permitted him to make. Now it was his to go out there, face the mountain, and maybe see if he could be of some help to Islaen Connor.

To his surprise, the Commando-Captain found Islaen standing with her back to the Dragon. She was leaning forward on the railing, looking dejectedly in the direction of the invisible ocean.

He spoke her name softly so as not to startle her.

The Colonel acknowledged his presence at once and moved a little to one side to allow him to join her. *I couldn't sleep*, she said to explain her being outside at this strange hour. *A bit overtired, I suppose.*

It was the same with me.—I feared for a moment that the Dragon was rising up again.

No. It's peaceful enough, for the time being, at least. It looks like there's a great-grandmother of a storm going on up there, though.

She fixed her eyes on the place where the peak was. Light flickered and flashed there almost in a continuous stream. She felt no alarm. This was natural lightning, not the pyrotechnics of an eruption. *That'll put more water in the streams if there's rain with it.*

Aye, he responded, then his hand touched hers. *You were troubled when I came out here. Will you let me try to help?*

Once more, the woman turned toward the sea. *I played the tyrant with Strombol tonight.*

You did no more than need demanded! I was hardly gentler.

I created a precedent, Varn. Every time such an incident occurs and succeeds, a similar example is set.—Do you realize how easily this privilege, if such dire responsibility can be so termed, can be abused?

Never shall it be while the Federation is led by officers like you.

It would take but one sport . . .

Islaen Connor, you cannot carry the whole universe, nor is it your place to try.

She smiled faintly. *It's a habit I picked up from a certain Arcturian officer.*

Her whole body suddenly tightened. *Listen to that mountain! The rumbling never stops now, as if the Dragon itself were caoining for those soon to die . . .*

She gripped herself. *I'm sorry, Varn. My thoughts are morbid tonight.*

Not morbid. You have the gift of putting words to the spirit of a situation.

He put his arm around her. *At least there is no ash falling at the moment, and the air is quite clear.*

Aye. It's coming in from the sea.

Sogan looked around the spaceport at the quiet starships, each sheltering her peacefully sleeping crew. His gaze came to rest on the *Jovian Moon.*

Our poor friends, he said with a sympathetic laugh. *It is a strange honeymoon they are having.*

I know, Islaen agreed. *It's a pity. You could feel their happiness when we planted . . .*

That has hardly altered, Colonel. They take delight in each other. He paused. *I am glad for that. They deserve it, the both of them.*

They deserve a bit of peace, too.

He smiled. *They are not doing too badly, Islaen Connor. Apart from some tedious hours spent scanning Tamboran records, their services have been in very little demand. We are the ones who have visited the local brass and done all the climbing and sailing, and poor little Bandit has spent her days dangling from the ceiling up in the High Monastery. —I take it none of this was entirely by accident?*

Not entirely, she admitted, smiling faintly herself. *We spent our first days together battling pirates. I didn't want to do the same to them.*

I figured as much.

He looked down at her. *Do you ever wish for peace, Islaen? Not just for a few weeks on furlough, but permanently? We have not known that, either of us, not since our youth.*

Sometimes, aye, but I don't think it's for us.

The War so marred us that we are no longer fit for it?

She twisted around so that she could look up at him. *No,* she answered slowly. *No, not that either. If we found something important enough and challenging enough, we could both be happy and fulfilled, but neither of us could ever walk away from our present work, not completely. We know what it means to the very survival of vast areas of the rim and maybe of the Federation itself, and we know it'll remain essential for a very long time to come. It's simply not in us to let it go ourselves and leave it to other hands. —We're not only superbly trained fighters, my friend, we're also endowed with superbly acute consciences to drive us.*

SIXTEEN

THE STORM SHROUDING the mountaintop held through the following day. It spread somewhat, scattering rain on the lower slopes and a little on Strombolis and the spaceport, enough to turn the ever-present ash into an unpleasant cement-gray crust, but for the greater part, it remained confined to the peak area.

There was no need to study the port meteorologist's report to realize that an incredible volume of water was being dropped on the summit. Every one of the normally tiny streams on that part of the mountainside visible to them was a raging torrent readily discernible without the aid of distance lenses.

It was better to see them so, Bethe Danlo thought. They seemed fair that way, kin to countless others cascading down heights on planets without number throughout all the ultrasystem. Lenses revealed their true nature far too clearly. They showed the vast amounts of dead and broken vegetation, the boulders and huge trunks most of them carried, the great clots of ravaged topsoil and coagulated ash.

Other things were present as well, but the distance was too great and the material involved too small for even the sensitive glasses to reveal the carcasses of the creatures slain by the rushing water or earlier by the fouled air, although she knew they were washing downstream in considerable number.

All the rivers were well above their normal levels, and only the extraordinarily deep gorges they had cut for themselves kept them from creating havoc throughout the whole island.

Those cuts still provided good leeway, but even they might prove insufficient if the precipitation kept up much longer at this rate. She did not know how much more water the miniature canyons could take before flash flooding became a real threat, especially if some of the debris lodged to create temporary dams.

The spacer said as much to Islaen, who was her only companion in their headquarters office.

She nodded in agreement. "We'd best send Strombol a warning of potential flood danger and tell him to see to his people."

"That's hardly necessary, is it? They're well familiar with that threat and aren't likely to miss recognizing it now."

Their own observations bore that out. The lower buildings near the stream bisecting Strombolis had been evacuated since the previous evening and the alternate safety channels opened to carry off as much of the excess flow as possible.

"Send it all the same. The good Commissar will be trying his best to hang me high. No use in giving him ammunition for a negligence charge on top of everything else."

Her slate eyes fixed pensively on her commander. "You do have permission for all this, Islaen?"

"I do, though I'd probably be acting as I am anyway if my courage proved the equal of it." The Noreenan sighed. "There's no way of knowing the state of that before it's tested."

"I've never found yours lacking," Bethe said. "I'll contact the palace now, unless you have something else you'd rather have me do first."

"No, see to that. There really isn't anything more that we can do at the moment. The rest is up to the Dragon."

The storm lessened to the point that the volcano's peak was once more visible from the port in the short time needed for the Sergeant to transmit her message and return again to her commander.

Islaen Connor had gone back to her desk but looked up when she heard her come in. "Well?"

"Mission accomplished. He wasn't particularly grateful for our warning. The Commissar highly resented that we should think it necessary to remind him of his duty."

"Unless we failed to do so," Islaen said none too pleasantly.

"Doubtless . . . —Space!"

The Colonel spun about in her chair so that she, too, faced the window behind her desk.

She paled as her eyes centered on the peak.

The pressure of the ever-expanding lake coupled with the mild but frequent tremors and the shock of the recent detonations had at last proven too much for the stability of the basically loose material forming the upper quarter of the notch's wall. Even as they watched, it fractured, shattered, and was gone.

For one instant, a silver-black cliff hung poised there, then it plunged outward, away from the breached crater and down.

"Now we've bought it," whispered the spacer as she followed its fall in frozen horror.

"Get to the roof! It may spread enough that the height will help!"

Islaen looked back over her shoulder at the onrushing doom. "Hold!"

Her voice shook a little, but she was unaware of that. "Hold up. It's turned. We're out of it."

The water wall had settled into the channel of one of the Dragon's rivers, and the flood, finding itself thus guided, merely followed the course laid out for it, one that would mercifully carry it away from both city and port.

The wave was no longer water, had not been almost from the moment it had torn from the destroyed lake. Its fury had stripped the slope and gorge of everything but the stark bedrock, turning the flood into a steaming slurry studded with boulders, some of them weighing more than fifty tons, and other debris.

It retained the characteristics of the lighter liquid, however, enough so that it compressed in the narrow places, towering at times to over ninety feet in height. It moved with awesome speed, covering the distance to the sea in a matter of minutes.

Islaen released the breath she had been unconsciously holding. "Find out who might have been within the path of that thing and get rescue parties out."

Her mouth hardened. Anyone caught directly by the slide had no need of saving, or of burial, either. He had been swept into Tambora's ocean or else lay beneath nearly one hundred feet of boiling mud.

* * *

All the short remainder of that morning and for most of the afternoon, a hushed stillness lay over the Tamboran spaceport, then loud, angry voices shattered the awed peace.

What now, Varn Tarl Sogan wondered wearily. He had stopped at Patrol headquarters to check on the slide damage reports. He was tired, and he did not regard the prospect of finding himself embroiled in some sort of on-world altercation with any degree of pleasure.

"Yeoman Baalbeer, find out what is going on."

"Aye, sir."

The Avian was soon back. "Some of the planters are here, sir. They're in heavy argument with the spacers. Captain Zubin seems to be leading our folk, and he looks as if he's about ready to flame the locals."

"Get the whole pack in here before he does. The last thing we need right now is a war."

"In here? There's a lot of them . . ."

"Here my authority will be instantly owned, outside, maybe less immediately so."

The voices rose higher in pitch. "Move now, before there is trouble for a fact. —Sergeant, Lland, go with her."

The Arcturian was scowling darkly by the time the Patrol agents returned with their charges. It was not a mask. He had enough to concern him with the Dragon without having to put up with human intolerance as well.

"What is this all about?" he demanded as soon as all were inside and the door was closed behind them.

"These characters have kept us cooling our fins for weeks," the Malkite master replied, shouting to make himself heard above the general rumble that answered the question. "Now they're scared that their precious crops are going to get fried or buried, so they're anxious to start delivery."

He glowered at the on-worlders. "Well, they're a bit too late! We're going to lift. We mightn't be as lucky a second time as we were this morning, like those two plantations in that flood's path weren't lucky."

He faced the Commando. "You said you'd back us, Sogan."

The Tamboran who appeared to be the spokesman for the planters gave the big spacer a contemptuous look but waited for the Captain's acknowledging nod before speaking himself. When he did, his voice was moderately low.

"They cannot lift. They are contracted to us, and according to your own interstellar law . . ."

Varn silenced him with a wave of his hand. "A starship's master is responsible for his crew and his vessel above any nonliving cargo, and he need not bring them into danger unless he has specifically chartered to do so. That, too, is interstellar law and is the more binding principle in this case."

He eyed the man and his fellows coldly. "You called this problem down on yourselves. Had you made delivery when the ships planeted, your crops would long since have been safely away, but you chose instead to make a display of the lack of importance off-worlders have for you by keeping their crews waiting like so many beggars. Now, you are just going to have to bear the cost of your contempt.

"Partial cost," he amended. "We will do what we can to secure disaster compensation for you, but I am well-nigh certain that no Federation judge will grant you anything like full value."

His eyes swept those before him. "I do understand that these charters are important to all of you, to the starships as their business, to you others because they represent your share, Strombolis' share, of the required port expenses. Their loss would represent a stiff hardship for both parties, and a compromise may still be possible."

He looked at Zubin with a faint smile. "Can you lade cargo in space, Captain?"

The huge man grinned. "Ask if we know how to steer the *Rounder* back to Malki!"

The other masters nodded their agreement.

"Hold your ships in orbit," Sogan told them. "The port has two shuttlecraft. They can ferry the stuff out to you, but one member of each crew will have to remain on-world to check out and sign for the shipments as if this were a normal delivery. Are you willing to do that?"

There was little hesitation before the spacers gave their assent. A certain amount of risk was too much a part of their work for them to balk long at this.

The war prince looked to the knot of Tamborans. "It is acceptable to you as well?"

"It is," the spokesman answered stiffly.

"I suggest you begin as quickly as possible. Your Dragon may terminate the operation rather suddenly."

He dismissed both groups with that, sending Abana Janst with them lest hostilities begin afresh outside.

The Malkite delayed a moment by the Arcturian's desk. "For brass, you're all right, Sogan," he remarked when the others had gone out of earshot.

He turned to leave with that but stopped when the Yeoman on duty in the communications room came to the door.

"More trouble," the agent told Varn. "That was Strombol. A lot of the fauna's come off the mountain and invaded the inland portions of the city, including fur snakes. There have been several fatalities already. Since we have the only weapons in Tambora, he wonders if we'd mind clearing them out."

"Send details off. Set them around the port as well. If those things are in Strombolis, they will not be much longer in reaching this far."

"We've got plenty of liquid fuel," Zubin suggested. "Ring the whole place with a good, wide layer of that, and none of them'll even try to get in."

"No way!" the Captain said sharply. "If that mountain starts shooting bombs—white-hot rocks or blobs of lava—the whole place would go up."

"It might anyway," the Patrol agent said slowly. "The reservoirs are well shielded and reinforced, but if they should be breached and ignite, there won't be enough of the spaceport left to identify. Even a fuel escape would be deadly. It'd be sure to go into the sea and take fire there. Any boats it caught might as well be in a star's heart for all the hope they'd have."

"Aye, I had been thinking about that myself. If the Dragon's activity increases any further, we may have to order the evacuation to begin at once."

The Malkite had listened to this exchange. Now he shook his head. "Why get so worked up? —Let me finish," he added, short-circuiting the anger he saw rise in both. "I know. It's your job, and you have to do everything you can to stop that mountain from killing us all, but I don't think you can completely outguess it and block every possible road to disaster. If you try too hard, you'll just as likely as not forget what volcanoes do best, blow themselves and everything around them to bits. Do what you can, and just chance the rest. That's what it'll come down to anyway."

He frowned. "I didn't say that right. I have no gift with words. What I mean is, if you get caught up in too many details . . ."

"I know what you mean."

Sogan's shoulders straightened. "That must be our concern. You have plenty of your own right now."

The former Admiral glanced toward the door. "You had best see to whatever arrangements you have to make with the Tamborans."

"Aye, Captain."

Zubin caught himself. Malkite spacers had little love for taking orders from anyone not of their own kind, and here he found himself docilely obeying this guerrilla.

He shrugged in his mind. Any fool knew that a starship did not need two masters in a crisis. He considered himself a good judge of men, and if anyone alive had a right to give commands and expect to have them heeded, Varnt Sogan did.

An explosive clap reached Varn as if from a very great distance, and he forced his eyes open, hoping as he did so that the disturbance was but part of his dreams.

It was not. A second shattered the stillness of the night even as he sat up and began pulling on his boots.

His head felt heavy and ached badly, the legacy of the ever-rising concentration of fumes he was forced to breathe.

Islaen?

I'm glad you're awake, Varn.

What is happening now?

The Dragon again. Come to the air lock.

The Arcturian joined his commander at the main hatch less than four minutes later.

To his surprise, he saw that she had partially withdrawn the picket, giving entrance to an uncommonly heavy ashfall.

Feel it, the woman instructed tightly.

Varn stretched out his hand. *Hot!*

In truth, it was only barely perceptibly warm, but his shock could have been little greater had it seared the flesh from his bones.

He gave the flame mountain a look of pure horror as yet another explosion rent the night.

Clap the viewers on that peak!

Already done, Admiral.

Islaen led the way back inside. No sooner had they reached the bridge than she set the picket back into place again.

Sogan did not notice. His eyes fixed and remained on the big viewer screen.

The scene revealed there was almost beyond comprehension. The crater was clearly visible, its encircling cliffs thrown into stark relief by the glare of the gigantic furnace that now crowned the much-grown infant cone he and the woman had first seen only days before.

The crest itself was clear even of mist, but great clouds loomed high over the Dragon, dark and heavy and alive with the play of lightning.

Farther down, the vegetation, also clearly visible in the lurid glow, was withered, dead, what little of it had not been flattened by the weight of ash. Two of the three fumaroles were terrifyingly alive, blazing in themselves and spitting gouts of fire so that only the heavy insulation provided by the ash blanket all around them prevented a major conflagration.

They were giving off more than fire. He could just make out thick, dark masses like gigantic ropes extending downward from each of them.

He frowned and drew closer to the screen in an effort to determine what they were.

The Noreenan saw him and studied the phenomena as well.

Lava, she said after several minutes. *It's moving so slowly that it's cooling and crusting over as it flows. That's why we can't see anything of the hot, liquid stuff inside.*

Her lips compressed. *In a way, it's too bad it is like this. The magma's too thick. If it were lighter, it might have served as a release for some of the pressure building within the Dragon. As it is, it'll stop too soon.*

The gurry was perched on the back of Islaen's flight chair, her feathers ruffled in her unhappiness. *Bandit's scared!* she whimpered.

"So are we all, love," the woman told her gently.

"I, for one, wish we could bolt at this point," Varn muttered.

Leave the city? Bandit asked.

"Aye, all of us on the island, small one. You cannot just abandon helpless people and seek safety yourself."

Nooo!

Islaen Conner barely heard them. She shook her head. It was coming so quickly, and the Navy was still three days or more distant . . .

Her resolution firmed. The burden lay with her and was not likely to be raised now. *Activate the transceiver. The evacuation must begin at once.*

It was but a matter of minutes before the Colonel made contact with Ivan Strombol, who, although he growled in protest and irritation at having been disturbed at such an hour, had no more been sleeping than was the off-worlder.

Islaen wasted no time. She told the Tamboran leader to begin the first phase of the withdrawal, that involving the children, the ill, and other particularly vulnerable members of the community.

Strombol gave her no answer for a number of seconds, and when he did, his voice was heavy with carefully studied doubt. "That may not be possible, Colonel. The Gray Ascetics have been conducting a powerful campaign against any such flight among the people . . ."

"Silence them."

"Such is not done on Tambora! Besides, they are men of enormous influence."

"Commissar," the Noreenan replied with a cold precision more gripping than any anger, "the only influence of any significance right now is the Dragon's. There's warm ash falling outside, as doubtless you are well aware. Farther upslope near the crest, it's coming down hot enough to blacken everything that was left alive up there, which was precious little. Had the force ejecting it been stronger or the wind driving it more powerful, we could well be receiving the same ourselves. How much longer can you expect our luck to hold?"

Her voice hardened. "We've had warning and warning in plenty, but that will not continue forever. Persist in ignoring what is plain for the seeing, and one day soon a great many Tamborans are going to die."

Once more, there was no immediate reply, but there was a

difference, an uncertainty, in the stillness this time, as if the Commissar had in that moment become aware in heart and soul of the reality of the threat that loomed over his people and city.

"Very well," he said at last. "The evacuation will proceed as you have instructed."

SEVENTEEN

PELE ROSE ON a scene out of nightmare.

Ash covered everything save where energy pickets had defended the starships. It was a foot thick in places and had drifted even deeper in odd corners, turning all the world gray and drear.

The mountain itself, once so marvelously alive and fair, was now desolation only. Nothing appeared to live beneath the heavy ash anywhere on the upper half, while on the lower slopes, where the damage was less extreme and the cover lighter, the few human dwellings hung on like condemned things awaiting the fulfillment of their doom.

The fires were gone, quenched since the early predawn, but something of the power that had given rise to them remained, for the two dark rivers still inched their slow way toward the sea, a goal neither would reach, although both had penetrated surprisingly far onto the inhabited slopes.

Their darkness stood in sharp contrast to the paler ruin around them, and the irregularities of the land over which they flowed had so shepherded them that they drew and held every eye that ranged up the slopes. A sharply ascending rise, a miniature hill, had turned their flow, sending one to the right, the other left of it so that they made a full circle around it before uniting to continue downward as a single stream.

The view below was no more comforting. The ocean itself had been marred. So great a quantity of ash had been cast upon it that huge gray mats now floated there, surrounding the few remaining boats. They might almost have been moored on land by the look of them.

Fortunately, the sludge was a surface scum only and offered no impediment to movement . . .

Islaen Connor tore her eyes away from the window. She had work to do and little enough time in which to accomplish it.

Varn, tell the spacers to lift, she told her comrade: *I want the evacuees assigned to them off-world now. Send the Patrol cruiser up as well. Joab can handle her alone.*

Those going were all port personnel. She could not trust the Tamborans not to panic in so alien a situation and could not risk putting the ships' crews in danger through them.

Her order did not include the shuttlecraft or the *Fairest Maid* and *Jovian Moon.* They would go only at the end, when all others were away and her company along with the Patrol unit and those others staying until the end were at last free to seek safety themselves.

Varn, she said suddenly.

He turned. *Aye?*

I just haven't thanked you for the way you handled that business between the spacers and those planters.

He shrugged. *I was wishing you were there to take over on that one.*

I wouldn't have done as well as you. For one thing, I'd never have thought to load from space. That was a brilliant stroke. Besides, the spacers respect you. The Colonel eyed him slightly less warmly. *They also thoroughly enjoyed your treatment of the Tamborans. —Be careful your dislike of them doesn't get us into trouble. We're working on a very fine surface as it is.*

My behavior toward them was correct, he told her stiffly.

Scrupulously correct, she agreed. *I know. I heard several delighted accounts of it.*

I think I know enough not to endanger our mission, Colonel Connor.

You've never done that yet, my friend. —Go on now. Finish up as quickly as you can.

He nodded and hastened to comply, leaving Jake with Islaen to help her with the final rush of administrative detail.

Once he had gone, the Colonel ordered that rebreathers be issued to the port staff who would remain longest and who were slated for the most strenuous activity.

She wished heartily that there were enough to supply them

all. The air was getting foul between its high particle content and the frequent, heavy influx of volcanic gases. It had already killed three people in Strombolis and seriously disabled another dozen. Several hundred more were beginning to experience respiratory difficulty, although they had not as yet suffered actual damage, and there was no one not having discomfort because of it.

She was not immune to that herself. Her throat was constantly raw and sore, and her lungs felt full, as if the airways were blocked, sometimes so much so that it was painful to draw breath, and always the muscles of her chest ached with the constant and growing effort to keep inhaling the tainted gas. Conditions had deteriorated to the point that she had confined Bandit to the filtered atmosphere of the *Maid*, much as her talent could have benefited them during the ordeal ahead.

Bad as all this was, it was still endurable, but ever with her was the fear that the air might turn from its present unpleasant but usable state into some lethal mixture before the evacuation could be completed.

The withdrawal was well on and was progressing with surprising rapidity. Ivan Strombol's acceptance of the danger threatening his people might have come late, but he responded to it now with determination and efficiency. The sense of urgency on him communicated itself to those he commanded, and that, coupled with the regimentation normal to their lives, kept the Tamborans moving quickly, without confusion and with little of the protest Islaen had been anticipating even before she had learned of the Gray Robes' campaign against her order. There was no panic.

Time was against them, that and the lack of ships necessary to carry off so large a number of people.

Many vessels had responded to the Commissar's call, but all were small, and all of them depended upon sail and oar to bring them the sometimes considerable distance to the various refuge ports. There was a significant delay between each run, and not every ship was able to return in time to take her place when the ragged fleet reassembled to prepare for the next.

Several journeys would be necessary before everyone could be taken off the imperiled island. Islaen had estimated four would be required in all and had set her departure orders accordingly.

Both the first and second waves had already gone, made up almost entirely of Tamborans. Only those off-worlders perceptibly weakening under the constant exposure to the gases had sailed with them, but the Commando-Colonel had made good her promise to reserve ships for the spaceport staff in the third run, now departing from the harbor. Half were leaving with that; the rest would go with the next and last. Part of the Patrol would be with them. The others would lift in the *Moon* at the very end.

The woman did not repent of her stubbornness in this matter. Off-worlders and Tamborans were equally her charge, and once the children and other more helpless individuals had been secured, she was not minded to give the city-dwellers any priority over the rest.

Indeed, she dared not do so. Strombol was an honest man and was not likely to purposely bring about another's hurt, but she put no trust at all in the Gray Ascetics. They possessed considerable influence, which the strangeness and fear of the moment was likely to intensify, and they viewed off-worlders as the major threat to their race, greater by far than the dire menace of the Dragon. If the port people all chivalrously waited until last, it was just possible that they might find their rescuers had suffered a regrettable delay in returning for them. That would not occur with a far larger number of native citizens still waiting to be taken off as well.

To further insure that there would be no treachery, she had stipulated that the Commissar himself, his chiefmost ministers, and all Ascetics, Red and Gray, not numbered among the ill should also wait until the final group was ready to depart. Even if her concern with actual betrayal was groundless, as was probably the case with this people, she thought the Tamboran sailors would exert themselves more strenuously for their own kind and leaders than they would for strangers alone.

Islaen closed her eyes for a moment to rest them. She had just gotten back from the docks after seeing the last of the third-wave ships off. There had been no trouble, as there had been none during the previous two runs, but still it was necessary for some of her company or of the Stellar Patrol unit to be present. A disturbance, however innocently begun, could too easily bring death or injury to a large number of people.

It was not pleasant work. Just being outside, in full sight and hearing of the angry mountain, was trying for body, mind, and spirit alike, and she had to contend with the decidedly unfriendly transmissions of those around her, those she was striving so hard to save. They were not enemies as she usually defined the term in her work, but most of them were very much unfriends.

Not surprisingly, the heaviest hostility came from those clad in somber gray robes, and she monitored them closely. All they had to do was pull their rebellion now . . .

There was no trouble. Their Abbot saw that his campaign to thwart the evacuation had failed, and he prudently held off creating any difficulty during the course of it, knowing he stood too great a risk of losing the following he needed to gain his eventual ends.

The guerrilla sighed, and for a moment, she was filled with a loathing for all her race. Here they were, battling under the threat that the Dragon would momentarily blow them all to atoms, and she had to squander her energy worrying about the quarrels of these isolationists.

She had just bent her head over her desk when Jake hurried inside. Something in his haste sent a chill through her, and she looked up sharply. "Trouble?"

The redhead nodded grimly. "We've just heard from the Commissar. Someone's trapped on that island in the lava."

"What!"

Islaen was on her feet and had crossed the room before he could begin any explanation. She had caught up her lenses from the desk and brought them to her eyes as soon as she reached the window.

It took a moment to focus, but then a small figure appeared clearly in the distance viewers.

It was a child, a boy of about six or seven. He was in the very center of the rise, at its highest point, and was looking about him in open terror. His face was streaked with ash and tears, and hopeless fear was visible in his expression.

"What's that baby doing up there?" she demanded.

"According to Strombol, his parents are followers of the Gray Robes. They determined to thwart the evacuation, at least

with respect to their own family. Since the children were to go
first, they hid the boy there and intended to slip away later,
after they had shown themselves around Strombolis to avert
any suspicion. Once they had joined him, they planned to hide
out in one of the abandoned monasteries. They figured no one
would miss them in the general upheaval until it was too late to
do anything about it.

"They never anticipated that their Commissar would truly
cooperate with us or the speed with which everything moved as
a result. They found themselves short of time to begin with,
and when dawn came and they discovered the rise surrounded
so that they couldn't get to it, they panicked. They held on this
long hoping the flow would stop and cool enough for them to
make a dash for it, but now they're being summoned to prepare
for the fourth run, and their hopes of rescuing their son
themselves fell so low that they finally went to Strombol in
desperation.

"He promptly came to us," he concluded with no good
grace.

Islaen seemed not to hear him. "I'll need a protection suit,
goggles for both the boy and me, a couple of rebreathers, and
one of the rovers. Fix up a suit for him as well as you can,
too."

The flier would have solved the problem readily for them,
but it had been sent out as part of the evacuation fleet and
would not be available again for several hours. By then, it
would probably be too late.

"What in space are you thinking to do?" asked the man
sharply.

"Go up there and get him, of course."

She studied the area through the lenses. "I'll drive as far as
the end of the flow. The ash won't let a rover go farther than
that, but I should be able to reach the top of it from the roof.

"If the crust will support me, I'll walk up it to the island,
slap the gear on the boy, pick him up, and carry him back
down."

"Is that all?" the Captain demanded sarcastically. "It's a
mad chance to take merely to go near that mountain, and your
odds for success . . ."

"Would you prefer for me to just leave him there, not to try
at all?" she snapped.

The Colonel gripped herself. "If my plan doesn't work, we'll have to wait for the flier's return, but I doubt the child will be able to hold out so long. Conditions have to be ghastly up there, and he looks so tiny . . ."

Islaen's shoulders squared. "Get yourself rigged out as well. I'll need a driver at the very least if I'm to bring an injured, terrified little boy down, and maybe other help as well. If I can get him as far as the rover, I don't want to blow it all there."

The blue eyes studied her in some amusement. "I'm flattered, Colonel Connor, but I wonder how pleased our Admiral will be when he finds I've been chosen over him for this jaunt."

She gave him a cool glance. "You're still the better on-world. He knows that."

"And doesn't take to the fact one bit."

"You count yourself a pretty good pilot. Do you enjoy standing up like a stark amateur next to him in space?"

The man winced. "That was a low blow, Colonel."

"Don't I have problems enough without having to play with my own colleagues' inflated egos?" she demanded bitterly.

"Colonel," Karmikel replied in great good humor. "Your far-famed consort will probably cut me into neutron-sized pieces for allowing you to take this on, forgetting entirely that no one can turn you from anything you've set your mind to do. Don't try to stop me from enjoying myself a bit at his expense first."

"And at mine as well," she said sourly. "Come on and get ready, you space tramp. With any luck at all, I won't have to risk you, either, but you might at least be prepared to face the worst."

EIGHTEEN

ISLAEN CONNOR RAN her tongue over her lips as she studied the lava flow.

Its surface was dark and rough and looked to be solid, but in her heart, she did not trust it. Of a certainty, she did not want to test it by driving the full force of her weight suddenly down on a tiny portion of it by springing onto it from the roof of the rover.

Perhaps she should try climbing it after all, she thought. It was hot, but the protection suit would shield her from at least serious burns if she took care not to rip it badly.

Jake realized what was holding her back and hastened to clamber up beside her on the top of the vehicle.

"I'm sorry, Islaen. I must be getting as dense as a white dwarf. —Lean on me while you swing onto it."

The woman looked at him a bit doubtfully but then nodded. The redhead's strength should more than be the equal of that.

So it proved, but even with his taking the most of her weight during the critical moment of contact, she felt the crust give slightly beneath her feet.

A sickening knot tightened in her stomach, but Islaen used her will savagely to quell the surge of fear. She was past the first hurdle. The surface had held and was likely to hold now for its full length. Unless it were softer up closer to its source or held weak spots, invisible to the eye and deadly . . .

Once more mastering herself, she raised her hand in salute to Karmikel and turned to begin her perilous trek.

Islaen quickly realized that her first impression of instability was not amiss. Although the flow was nearly halted and was, presumably, cooling, its core was still molten very nearly to the surface, more than near enough to keep the crust very slightly plastic.

Her brows came together beneath the shielding goggles as a powerful sensation of familiarity filled her. This had happened before . . .

She remembered. Once when she was a child, when the little pond near her home had frozen over, she had ventured out on it. The slick surface had wobbled so just before it had shattered under her.

A violent shudder ran through her. All that had happened then was a soaking to the knees in the frigid water and a long lecture from her parents on the danger of what she had done. The breaking of this would be another matter altogether.

Her eyes closed. She had faced death so often, in so many different forms, but she did not wish to meet her end this way. Just the thought of what lay only inches beneath her feet, this river out of the wellsprings of Noreen's chief hell, was enough to freeze the breath within her breast.

Once more, she forced her mind to calm, but it was only to find that she was in truth having trouble drawing air. Within minutes, the volume of gas reaching her had fallen to a bare trickle insufficient to maintain life.

The Noreenan ripped off the rebreather she was wearing. She gagged. The stuff she had instinctively drawn into her starving lungs stank with sulfur and with the strange, pungent smell of very hot rock.

Cursing her stupidity in not properly checking out her equipment before starting on such a mission, she put on the extra one, that intended for the boy. She winced at its tightness but did not delay to adjust its bindings. There might be little time to spare as it was when she did reach the child.

Quickening her pace as much as she dared, the Commando hastened up the steep slope. Ash was beginning to come down again. It was light as yet, but she did not look forward to making the return in a heavy storm of it such as those they had been experiencing most recently.

At last, she reached the island.

The extraordinarily sharp rise of the land worked with her, and she was able to leap from the lava to it without giving any severe jarring to the treacherous surface. She stumbled upon striking the ash-laden ground but soon regained her balance and began the climb to its crest.

Islaen made it quickly and without incident. A little too quickly. The small Tamboran huddled close to the boulder he had vainly been trying to use for shelter and stared at her with a terror greater than that with which he regarded the nightmare world all around him.

The woman realized that, apart from the fact that she was patently an off-worlder, she must present an appalling image, masked as she was with defensive gear and filthy with ash and sweat.

She hurriedly lifted the goggles and removed the rebreather, this time taking care to inhale very shallowly so that the sudden change in air should not set her choking.

"Don't be afraid," she said calmly. "Commissar Strombol himself wanted me to come up for you."

"The Commissar? For me?" The boy's expression had changed to one of amazement.

Islaen nodded. "Aye. Your parents were worried about you and told him you were here, so he called me. He cares about all Strombolis' citizens, you know."

"But—but you are from the spaceport!"

"I'm with the Federation Navy. I care about people, too. —Here, put these things on. They won't fit very well, I'm afraid, but it's the best we could do on short notice. They'll protect you from the heat on the way down."

She helped the child to dress, carefully fastening the garments and tying on the boots and gloves. Last of all, she put on and adjusted the goggles and rebreather.

Islaen Connor had to fight to keep her hands from shaking. The poor little fellow! His face, hands, and neck, especially the latter, were raw and bleeding from the buffeting of the ash.

"Do your eyes hurt?" she asked gently, concealing her fear.

"No, not much. I used to put my head down in my arms like this when it started blowing badly. There—there was not much to look at anyway."

That explained why his neck was comparatively so badly cut. The Tamboran had managed to keep the rest covered during the worst of it.

"That was good thinking, lad." She paused. "What's your name, by the way?"

"Ruger Ecks."

"Are you ready to try an escape, Ruger?"

"I am," the Tamboran replied with a surprising show of spirit.

For the first time, the Commando hesitated. She had intended to carry the child down, but the lava crust had felt so unstable that she feared even so much additional weight might be enough to puncture it.

She studied the boy carefully. He was bearing up under his ordeal with a great deal of courage. Would it be enough to bring him through?

"Ruger, can you aid me? I was going to carry you, but my rebreather's broken, and I don't think I'll be strong enough to take you down. Do you think you can go by yourself, walking beside me?"

The young Tamboran lifted his head. His eyes sparkled proudly behind his goggles at the thought that he should be allowed to take an active part in his rescue. "Aye."

"Very well then. I'll lift you onto the flow and follow after. It's hot there, but your boots will see that you don't get burned. You'll have to be sure you don't fall and tear your clothes or do any jumping or heavy stepping. Otherwise, we should be fine."

"I shall be careful," Ruger assured her gravely.

In all too short a time, they had reached the place where the lava flow approached the solid ground of the rise most closely. There was only a very little space separating the two sites at that point, and Islaen felt they could make the transition without putting too great a stress on the crust.

She lifted her charge onto it and, after warning him to stand well away, made her own move.

In order to equalize her weight, she went to her knees and crawled out upon the flow. The heat of it brought tears to her eyes, but the protection suit shielded her well enough in the short time she was down that she knew she had taken only minor burns, nothing that should cripple her.

The boy hurried to her once she was on her feet again. This eerie, hot place filled the Tamboran with fear, but he was somehow managing to hold it in check.

Islaen Connor smiled at the small, begoggled face looking

up at her and held out her hand. "Let's go, Ruger. We'll hold each other up."

It was a hard trip despite its shortness, very hard for the guerrilla. The ash came down heavily, and a strong, ever-changing wind whipped it against her so that her lips and lower face were soon bleeding from its constant grinding. Her mouth and throat felt parched, and she battled to suppress the urge to cough lest she risk doing to her lungs what was happening to her skin.

Before they had gone a quarter of the way, she longed for water and longed unutterably for a breath of pure, untainted air.

The Commando pressed on grimly, knowing that if she weakened visibly now, the little Tamboran might shatter completely. Ruger was so young to have undergone such an ordeal, and he had borne it for many hours already.

When they finally reached the rover, Islaen stared numbly at it, for an instant scarcely recognizing it or its significance, but she recovered herself in the next moment and helped ease the child into Jake Karmikel's welcoming arms.

Seconds later, she felt the redhead's firm, steadying grasp. There was one fearsome instant as she passed from the lava flow to the roof of the vehicle, then she slumped against the Captain, safe and free of the nightmare at last.

Her eyes closed with relief as she slid into the rover. The climate conditioning felt marvelous to heat-tormented skin, and the luxury of breathing the filtered air was a pleasure so exquisite as to be almost painful.

For now, she could relax, rest and enjoy this release. Her comrade had the controls, and for the next few minutes, she could surrender all responsibility for their lives into his capable hands.

NINETEEN

THE OXYGEN-RICH air speedily revived the woman, and she soon lifted her goggles and those of the boy. She released his rebreather a moment later.

Ruger winced several times during the brief operation but made no complaint.

Islaen gently touched his smudged, scratched cheek. "I'm sorry to have hurt you. We'll have you fixed up fast once we get you under a renewer back at the infirmary."

She sighed to herself. The regrowth would be needed as well if Ruger's lungs had taken significant damage, and she did not see how the child could have escaped that, not with the hours of exposure he had endured.

She made no attempt to question him, however, and endeavored to keep her tone light, not wishing to put any further fear on him. A few minutes' treatment would set everything aright again.

Jake, too, maintained an air of complete normalcy. He casually tossed a first-aid kit back to the Colonel. "You'd better do what you can with that before we reach the city. You're a right pair of beauties the way you are."

Islaen made quick use of the coagulant stick on both of them and then handed her small companion a jar of washing cream.

Ruger scowled at it. Now that the immediate danger was past and nearly all the discomfort was gone, he was reluctant to give up entirely the marks of his adventure.

The Noreenan man smiled. A coating of grime would not have troubled him, either, at that age. "Scrub away, lad," he

147

advised. "Your parents are scared half off their circuits now, and if they see you looking like this, it'll finish the job."

The cream was designed to work rapidly and efficiently, and both were soon as presentable as was possible for them to be before a renewer ray could be turned on them.

Ruger became very quiet. With nothing further to occupy his attention, he had begun to study his immediate surroundings and had suddenly realized that he was riding within one of the much-condemned spaceport vehicles. Not only that, it was moving fast, jerking every now and then with the irregularities of a road that seemed all too threateningly steep.

He turned to his rescuer, and once again, the Colonel guessed the cause of his alarm. "Don't worry. Jake can fly a starship, so I think we can depend upon him to pilot a little rover for us."

The remaining residents of the city and the off-worlders alike had watched the vehicle's progress, and when it began the last phase of its descent, most of those still present on the island gathered at the spaceport gate.

The rover came to a stop near the entrance, and Islaen stepped out of it, carrying the boy in her arms.

A cheer greeted their appearance, but when she tried to approach the waiting medics, several Tamborans moved to block her way. The man leading them was clad in gray, and his robe stood out from most of those of his kind in that it was bordered at its hem with brilliant orange. The Abbot himself.

"We will take the child," the Gray Robe declared.

Islaen Connor eyed him coldly. "After our physicians have finished with him."

"He has suffered defilement enough already."

"You don't have so much as a renewer, much less a regrowth ray. He needs the one and maybe the second as well."

"What Tambora lacks, a Tamboran must forgo."

For a moment such anger flared on the Noreenan that those facing her gave ground a few paces, and even Karmikel was startled by the vehemence of the emotion she was not bothering to conceal.

"This valiant Federation citizen is not going to suffer any neglect. Now get out of my way!"

Most obeyed, but three including the Ascetic leader still held firm.

Islaen could feel Ruger trembling in her arms as the boy buried his face against her shoulder.

That seemed to infuriate the Abbot. "Give us the child!"

A flash of blaster fire exploded between them, and Varn Tarl Sogan stood beside the Commando-Colonel. "Had you gone up after him, you might have some say as to how to treat him," he hissed. "As it is, you are just in the way. Now move, you and these vermin with you! I shall not waste another charge. If I am compelled to fire again, it will be with effect."

The massive form of Zubin of Malki loomed next to the guerrilla Captain. "Clear, fast, you planet-hugging bastards, or I'll set you dancing!"

Ruger's grasp tightened around the Colonel's neck. "Oh . . ."

"It's bluff talk," she whispered, "but go with the physicians now, and let me take care of this. I don't want trouble between our peoples."

"Please hurry. He is the Gray Abbot."

"I know, lad."

She gave the boy over to the white-uniformed man nearest her. "Get him away from here fast, before his parents recover enough from their shock and relief to intervene. We couldn't shout them down as easily."

"Aye, Colonel."

Islaen turned back to the enraged men. "All right! That will be quite enough."

She raised her voice so that those standing farther from the group could also hear her. "If the boy's lungs are damaged, they will be quickly repaired. Should we deny him treatment, he might well be severely crippled for the remainder of his life, and that life would probably be drastically shortened as well. To permit any such easily prevented tragedy would be as bad as leaving him trapped by the lava. In both cases, I was morally bound to take the course I followed.

"Ruger will be returned to his parents once we're certain he's truly whole. In the meantime, you Tamborans, go back to your homes and, port personnel, to your work. You'll be summoned when enough of the boats return to begin boarding.

Right now, it's best not to stay out too long with the ash falling like this."

The crowd dispersed fairly quickly after that and in complete order, adroitly moved and channeled by the Patrol unit, so that soon only Sogan, Jake, Zubin, and a few others remained near the Colonel.

Islaen started to reenter the rover, but the breath relief caused her to draw was too deep, and she was seized by a fit of coughing of such violence that she was forced to lean upon the machine for support.

Everything seemed to fall into a strange blur of giddy movement as strong hands closed on her shoulders.

When the world cleared once more a few seconds later, she was resting on the rear seat of the vehicle with a mask pressed to her face forcing pure oxygen into her lungs.

"That'll hold her until the medics can get to work on her," the Malkite was saying.

Islaen twisted her head free. "No. No medics. I'm all right now. A little rest will fix me up fine."

"No way, Colonel," Varn told her tightly. "You must have swallowed a record dose of that poison up there."

"I can have that checked later, but now, the physicians would try to ground me. We can't afford that, not with the boats due back soon and tensions building."

Her companions were frowning. They knew she was right, but they were afraid for her, and afraid, too, what a second, real collapse at the wrong moment might mean.

"We shall take her to the *Maid*," Sogan said decisively. "If she requires further treatment after a turn under our renewer and some proper rest, we can get it for her then." Her own talent would be able to tell them if she needed that, and personally, he felt that a bit of quiet and some peace would soon bring her back to her own.

Zubin grinned. "Good enough. We can trust you to sit on her if anyone in the galaxy or beyond can do it."

"The *Fairest Maid* it is," Islaen Connor agreed wearily, pleased to have won her point so far and really too tired for further argument.

The effort of concentrating on the Malkite's words brought another question to her mind, and she straightened again.

"What are you doing here, Captain Zubin? You spacers are all supposed to be off-world."

"Didn't I prove handy just now?" the other countered.

"You did, but my question stands."

"Oh, the *Rounder* and my lads are safe in space. I just decided to stay on myself. I got to thinking that if half-sized hands like these two could be useful, so could a fine specimen of a man like myself. Besides, it was a matter of pride. I'd done so much talking about our right to lift that I was afraid folks'd get to imagining Malkites aren't much good when something unusual's going on."

The Noreenan shook her head. "Threatening that Gray Robe with a blaster . . ."

"Power down, Colonel! Captain Sogan threatened him a lot worse than I did. We didn't want to give him that little tadpole any more than you did, and you'd probably have done the same thing yourself if your hands hadn't been full. I didn't hurt him any. Besides, he was probably relieved that I only shot off my mouth instead of dusting the road with him. The Spirit of Space knows, that's what I was really itching to do."

"I'm glad you restrained yourself," Islaen said dryly. "Federation-Tamboran relations are strained enough right now without adding anything like that to the fuel mix. We'd probably all have wound up facing atrocity charges, if nothing else."

She would be lucky if she did not have those slapped on her anyway after this day's work, she thought glumly, for having taken Ruger without consulting his parents, but then she put the thought from her mind. She was too spent to worry about that now, and there were too many more immediate concerns before them all.

Varn watched the woman set down her cup. It was her third, but the water seemed finally to have slacked the thirst put on her by ash and heat, for she sat back at last in apparent contentment.

He sighed to himself. She seemed so tired.

She was hurting, too, or almost certainly had to be. The renewer had closed the surface lacerations and erased the light burns she had taken despite the protection suit, but Islaen's expedition on the lava had branded her more deeply than that.

She had been lucky and had escaped major injury, but she
needed a session under a regrowth and would have to have it
eventually, if only to avoid being left extremely vulnerable to
similar wounding in the future.

He absently broke off a portion of his supper for Bandit. The
gurry was the only one of them to retain her appetite. Islaen
had eaten nothing at all, and he had been able to force himself
to do only a little better. Everything seemed to taste of sulfur
or ash.

The Jadite mammal looked up at them after clearing his
offering. *Why won't Islaen and Varn let Bandit help? Bandit
doesn't want to stay here anymore!*

"You will stay, all the same," the Commando-Captain told
her severely.

"The air's too bad now, love, and you're too little for us to
fix up breathing equipment for you. It'd be too dangerous for
you to be outside without that."

But, Islaen . . .

"Not now, Bandit," Sogan warned. "She is too spent to
argue with you. If you want to remain part of this command,
you are going to have to obey our orders."

Yes, Varn.

The man settled into a rather glum silence after that.

His consort watched him for several seconds. *I'm sorry,
Varn,* she said softly, knowing full well what was bothering
him.

He shrugged. *I am enough of an officer to accept my
limitations,* he told her gruffly.

You're still hurt.

Aye.

Jake was just there, Varn. We had to move fast.

*You would have chosen him anyway, even had I been
standing beside him.* He looked away from her as he clapped
his mind shields into place. She knew he was wounded, but his
pride would not allow him to let her see how deeply. "When
am I going to be good enough to really help you, to share all
of your work fully, on-world as well as in space?"

The guerrilla leader bit her lip. "I have to use my unit to its
greatest efficiency, Varn."

"I know. I should do the same thing, but it still galls me that

Karmikel, that anyone, should be chosen to stand by you when I am not fit to do it."

"You've never done less than your part! Damn it, man, that row of stars you've managed to collect should be proof enough of that even for you!"

Varn Tarl Sogan sighed. "Stars? They prove that I have fought well. It is you . . . —Islaen, I shall never grow accustomed to seeing you go into danger, much less enjoy watching you do it. It is just somewhat easier when I am able to share it with you. At least, I do not have to feel so helpless, so worthless, then."

He straightened and forced his thoughts to open again. *Knock out while you have the chance*, he told her. *You must be feeling pretty rotten.*

That's an accurate enough diagnosis, Islaen admitted ruefully, *but . . .*

Go on, for a few hours anyway. I plan to do the same. The fourth run is nowhere near ready to start yet, and you will have to be back in something like normal shape to manage that. Bandit can keep watch and let us know if anything comes up.

TWENTY

VARN TARL SOGAN woke several hours later. He was not slept out, yet despite his weariness and the dull heaviness of his mind, he could not return to sleep.

He looked out through the cabin door into the hall beyond. The evening lights had been activated, so he knew darkness had fallen. They were dim, gentle to tired eyes, but still, he turned away from them and faced the wall, thoroughly annoyed with himself. Everything was quiet and peaceful with nothing at all amiss. There was no reason to be so on edge.

Varn frowned. There was a strange, soft buzzing in his head. Was he ill, he who had done nothing at all the previous day?

The clouds cleared from his mind. The odd little sound was not in his mind but in his ears, his ear that was resting upon the pillow. When he raised himself a bit, the noise vanished. When he returned to rest, it was there once more.

The Arcturian was dressed within a matter of seconds. Something was wrong, he feared in his heart, terribly wrong. If only Islaen had not yet sunk into too deep a sleep. He hated the thought of disturbing her, but she was the one who had been in deep conference with the volcanologists, and she might know what was happening now. He dreaded even the short delay that would result from the need to rouse her . . .

The Commando-Colonel was indeed in her bed, but she woke immediately at his call and touch.

Sogan quickly described the sound that had disturbed him. He felt no sense of embarrassment over making so much out of what seemed a very small thing, not with the horror looming

over all of them. Ignorance was the folly and shame in such a
case, not momentary overreaction to a mystery.

Islaen was on her feet before he had finished speaking. She
went to her desk, rested her head upon it. After a moment, she
dropped to her knees and, to his complete astonishment,
clamped her teeth on one of the metal studs bracing it.

When she again stood up, she was whiter than the former
Admiral had ever imagined any living creature could be.

*It's harmonic vibration, the sound of vast amounts of magma
in rapid motion very close to the surface—it wants out. Varn,
the Dragon's going to go, maybe within hours. Our time's just
about gone.*

Sogan accepted her statement with deadly calm. He had
anticipated this moment since he had seen that thrice-accursed
column of steam rising from the supposedly dormant mountain, and his fears had been confirmed in the Noreenan
woman's actions and appearance just now, before she had ever
spoken. Their part was clear, simple. Whether the mountain
would allow them the time necessary to complete their work,
that was beyond their knowledge or controlling.

The Commando-Colonel first contacted the fleet to inform
them of this latest development and then called Strombol.

She tersely explained what was happening. "Start loading
the boats at once," she concluded. "There should be enough in
the harbor now to carry most of us if each takes on her full
capacity."

"Sail at once?" Ivan asked.

His voice, too, was calm. With the culmination of the
emergency on him, he knew he must be his people's leader in
fact, perform as none in his long line before him save only its
famous founder had ever been compelled to do.

What he faced was worse. The first Commissar had brought
salvation to a colony nigh-unto slain by gross mismanagement.
Now, this city, this ancient city where Tambora's history had
begun, cowered before a foe more appalling than any mere
human hate or human weakness, the blind, irresistible fury of
a planet gone mad.

Islaen hesitated only the barest moment before answering.
"Aye, when five have been readied to go and every five boats
thereafter. Those craft are all too small to send them off
entirely alone so heavily laden and at night."

"It will be done as you wish."

The guerrilla thanked him and closed the transceiver.

She glanced at Sogan, who had remained with her while she had made both transmissions. *That's it, I suppose. You'd best ready the* Maid *for space.*

Karmikel can do that, he replied evenly.

Jake?

He nodded. *Bethe will prepare the* Moon *for him. We have arranged that already.*

Varn . . .

We will have to be at the docks before I could get half started myself.

Her great eyes seemed to darken. *She may have to lift fast.*

You need me. That Gray Abbot may try to avenge what he has to see as a defeat, and however much Strombol may recognize the need for cooperation between us in this crisis, he might not be able to do anything, especially not if he doesn't know there is a plot at hand until it is sprung. With our minds linked, I can also monitor our enemies' transmissions. At the very least, you do know you can depend on me not to bolt on you.

The Noreenan's head lowered. *Come, then. You know you're welcome.* She just prayed he would not regret his courage.

For his part, Varn Tarl Sogan was hard-pressed to hold his expression and the transmissions of his mind steady before her. He had gained his will, but nothing, not even his love and fear for this woman, could make him want to remain any longer on Tambora of Pele.

An icy hand seemed to close about his heart. It was superstition only, but he could not shake a dread that was well-nigh certainty that the Dragon hungered to take them for its victims, these two who had fought so hard to deny it any, whatever it might do or refrain from doing with the rest of Strombolis' populace.

The docking area looked strange, surrealistic, in the harsh, steady glare of the spaceport lights the Colonel had ordered set up there.

As before, everything was going smoothly, with small, quiet groups coming to the boats as they were summoned.

Most of the off-worlders were now afloat. She had sent them

into every second craft until only her own comrades, the Patrol unit, and those others who had agreed to stay to aid with crowd control and last-minute chores remained with her. These ones, too, would stay altogether should there not be sufficient boats or spacecraft to bring everyone away.

There was some danger of that last, although vessels continued to arrive in a steady trickle, and she had good cause to hope that enough would eventually come to insure all of them a place, that no one need be left standing in the doomed city when the last transport out was gone.

Islaen glanced toward the invisible, constantly roaring volcano.

Was there enough time? If only the Dragon would hold off long enough for them all to make their escape! If only she had not delayed too long before ordering the evacuation to begin . . .

"Colonel!"

The high, young voice broke into her bleak thoughts, and she looked around to see Ruger Ecks hurtling toward her, deftly avoiding the arms of the couple in whose company he had come and who now tried to intercept him.

Islaen caught and lifted him. "You're looking fit now, lad!" she said with a laugh. "I'm right glad to see you."

"I was afraid you would not be here. I heard a spacer telling one of the physicians that you were sick, too."

"I was a bit spent after we got back."

She set the child down. "Your parents seem about ready to board."

"Yes, but I did want to give you greeting."

"I'm happy you did. —Look after your kin and do what they tell you. That's important now. You've braved the Dragon and know enough not to want to do anything that might force them to have to face it as well."

"No, Colonel," he replied gravely, "I surely do not."

He gave a final wave and ran back to the two adults from whose side he had sped.

Bethe came up beside the Noreenan. She was smiling softly. "You were very good with him."

"The poor little fellow was through a lot. He held up so bravely and is so nice himself that it's impossible not to like him."

The demolitions expert sighed as the boat bearing the Tamboran family slowly moved away from her dock and out of the illuminated area. "He belongs in the stars. It's a crime before humanity that his life must be so circumscribed."

"There's more than one path to greatness and fulfillment, praise the Spirit of Space. He has it in him to make much of life, whatever course he follows."

"I sincerely hope you're right."

The spacer put the wistful mood from her. "How are we doing? There's been no trouble yet, but I keep thinking that merely means someone's planning a surprise for us."

"Aren't you the gloomy one!"

"Come on, Islaen! What kind of readings are you picking up from them?"

The other immediately grew solemn. "From what Varn and I can put together, we appear to be better accepted than at any time before. My going up the mountain and walking that lava flow to get Ruger seems to have won most of them, as has the fact that the boy likes me. Since children are relatively few here, they're precious, and people respond to genuine kindness and consideration toward them."

"Even your collapse probably helped us."

"It has. It was witnessed by quite a number and has gained me a store of sympathy since I was downed saving one of their own, especially as I still held to my feet to fight for him. The Tamborans appreciate that, apparently, even if they disagree with my sending him to the infirmary, and few seem to be objecting even to that. At least, that's about the way of it with the great majority."

"The rest?"

Her lips curled in distaste. "There's not many of them, but they're emitting strongly, and I don't enjoy picking up what they're sending out."

"Hate? Anger?"

She nodded. "Aye, both, but it's a collective emission with no real focus, not even Varn, who's managed to rankle a lot of them. —It's ugly, Bethe, unreasoning. The very fact that we're helping to save lives gives fuel to it."

"Well, we couldn't really expect gentle neutrality from our friend the Gray Abbot after that scene over Ruger."

"He, or one I believe to be him, is decidedly hostile to us," she agreed, "as are a few with him. That's actually a cleaner response than this other, though I fear it because it may well make them the more daring."

The Noreenan frowned. "There's a kind of triumph on them that I don't like or trust."

"With reason," the spacer agreed grimly, more troubled by this part of her Colonel's report than by any of what she had said before it. "The rest, I can accept, but anything pleasing to that crowd at the moment is likely to be detrimental to the rest of us."

Despite Bethe's forebodings, nothing occurred to delay the evacuation, and only a handful of people remained on the nearly empty dock when Pele's light again filled the sky.

The last of the boats had gone. A few of the on-worlders were left, some of whom were even now entering the rover that would take them to the spaceport. They and most of the remaining off-worlders would lift in the shuttlecraft. A few of the latter, Zubin and a couple of the Patrol-Yeomen, would go with the *Jovian Moon* shortly thereafter. Varn and Islaen would go last of all in the *Fairest Maid*.

It had been a close thing, Varn Tarl Sogan thought as he watched the final ships vanish over the horizon. Fear and unavoidable delay had reduced the number of vessels returning to the harbor this last time, but space had been found for everyone between them and the port craft.

They were leaving barely in time. For the past hour, the Dragon had been shaken by subterranean explosions so loud and constant that the ground beneath them trembled as though with fever, although as yet not violently, and low speech was nearly impossible because of the volume of the nearly continuous rumbling.

The Tamboran leaders were ready to leave for the shuttle.

He approached them. Islaen had left him with this part of it while she made certain the spaceport was clear. "You have confirmed that all your people are safely away?" he asked Ivan. "We do not want anyone dead through some oversight or snafu on our part."

"Strombolis is not so large that its bureaucracy has negated its humanity," the Commissar responded stiffly. "No one was forgotten."

"And your folk, Abbot?" he asked of the scarlet-clad man standing a little behind Strombol.

"We are all accounted for as well."

"What about yours?" the former Admiral demanded of the Gray Robe who was so strong a center of hostility against his party.

"All of us intending to go are either already away or here with me."

The Arcturian's eyes narrowed. "What do you mean?"

"Three neophytes of my community are determined not to desert their places despite alien will to the contrary. I could not gainsay them, and now that it is too late to thwart them, I am free to reveal their steadfast courage before all Tambora."

Varn Tarl Sogan's response was a sharp oath in his own tongue.

His head snapped toward Issicar Lland, who was standing beside him. "Yeoman, you brought the *Daber* here in case we should need her?"

"Aye, sir, despite her size, but . . ."

"Excellent. I can manage her alone."

"No!"

"The way that mountain is roaring, we cannot delay any longer. Your boat will hold the four of us should I be able to find those Gray Robes and get us far enough that you can come back and pick us up safely."

"You'll never have time, sir," the Lirman told him quietly.

"I must at least try. I cannot just leave them to die, poor, microwitted fools though they be."

Lland's head lifted. "You can't go alone."

"I have no time for heroics, Yeoman!" he snapped and then softened. "We cannot rightly risk more than one, and you are needed here. —Give me your energy cuffs. With their help and my blaster's, I should be able to roust those three out of their holes and bring them down in relatively short order."

His frigid eyes struck the Gray Ascetic. "In which monastery are they hiding, or have they split up?"

"My memory fails me . . ."

"Answer him, and answer him truthfully."

The Gray Robe whirled at Ivan Strombol's command. "Commissar?"

"You heard me."

The Abbot straightened. "I refuse. By my authority . . ."

"You have none, not civil and not moral. The one lies with me, the second with the heads of the Red Ascetics. You will obey me now and obey this off-worlder."

Strombol's look was one of contempt, of utter disgust. "Never before in all the history of Tambora has one so highly placed so betrayed his position or his honor or the essential beliefs of our people. It is the shame of every Tamboran that we share race with you!"

"What is my wrong?" the other demanded imperiously. "What have I done save refuse to condone the delivery of our people into alien ways?"

"The Dragon is active and an imminent peril to everyone on this island. Would you have had us all die rather than listen to and cooperate with these others?"

The Commissar's voice was thick with an anger his will was scarcely able to hold in check. "You hate this man who has thwarted your will and whom you see as responsible for your being bested yesterday, although yours was, in point of fact, entirely the doing of that.

"In order to avenge your pride against him, you have, at the very least, permitted three youths in your charge to enter into needless danger, if you didn't maneuver or actually order them to their stand, and you have put Captain Sogan into the same dire peril. Our race is not so withdrawn from all other life that you could not have guessed how a man of his caliber would have to react, most particularly since you have already witnessed some measure of his unit's courage and compassion.

"There are some who would put the name of attempted murder on what you have done, and I am one of them. If Captain Sogan or any of his people should choose to press charges against you before Federation court, no protest will be made on your behalf, and no Tamboran support will be given you. Rest assured of that. —Now, where are those boys?"

"In the High Monastery," the Gray leader replied sullenly. "They did not say where or how they would pass their time."

"I shall just have to search them out, then," the Commando said. "Unfortunately, that will probably mean the defilement of a large part of the place, rendering it unfit for further use by your kind. But that is hardly my problem."

He had not quite been able to keep the vindictiveness firing that statement out of his voice, and it was another moment before he could quell it, but he doubted anyone here was much inclined to judge him too severely because of it. They all knew as well as he that he was in all probability casting his life away; the Dragon was too obviously awake to permit any doubting that the crisis was now upon Strombolis and any mortal creature unfortunate enough or foolish enough to be within sight of it.

Sogan said little more. There was no need. Issicar Lland was well able to assume command of what remained of this part of the evacuation. In another couple of minutes, he was in one of the port rovers and speeding toward the city and the quickest route to the imperiled monastery.

Islaen Connor battled down her terror of the raging volcano as Varn's mind withdrew from hers. Ostensibly, he had but informed her of his decision to go up after the three Ascetics. In actuality, she knew he had been saying good-bye to her. The former Admiral did not anticipate either succeeding in this mission he had taken upon himself or returning from it.

Her own determination swelled within her. Her work in the spaceport was finished, and her charges were safe. All that remained was to take the *Fairest Maid* off-world, and that Jake could still do for her. He had not yet lifted in his *Moon*.

Speaking tersely into the communicator she wore on her left wrist, she told the Commando-Captain of the latest alteration in their plans and put him in command of the unit and the withdrawal. That done, she resolutely severed contact with him.

Her pride in the Arcturian war prince waxed hot and high. There was nothing redeeming, nothing appealing or even acceptable, about these Tamborans in his eyes, yet he had put himself into the awesome power of the flame mountain because three of their kind were in death peril from it.

He was not going to face that foe alone. Even the knowledge that his rescue attempt would almost certainly prove futile and would probably bring him to the same doom shadowing the three youths did not weaken her resolve. Those Gray Robes were no less hostile to him because of their age and present plight, and she, for one, did not trust them, not after what she had seen of their master. They might be glad of his coming after having lived alone with the Dragon's new fury for a while, but they might also be lunatics. There were many ways to encompass a man's death without having to do the physical deed oneself, far too many ways. She intended to insure that Varn Tarl Sogan should not meet with any of them, even if her own destruction be required of her as a result.

Yet another explosion rent the heart of the mountain, louder and sharper than of those preceding it, although it was still confined underground.

Fear was a sick force filling all her body and mind. The Dragon. The Dragon could too easily see to it that they never reached the small boat, that she never joined with the Arcturian at all.

Her head raised. No matter. She could at least send her soul to him. They might not be physically together when the Grim Commandant claimed them if that was to be their fate, but her husband would know that a friend was with him. He would not go into the dying alone.

TWENTY-ONE

VARN'S ROVER TORE upslope, keeping to its top speed despite the rugged, treacherous ground, and he knew a momentary feeling of gratitude that the spaceport had not been stocked with more delicate, civilian-type labor vehicles. A run like this would have completely defeated almost anything save these ultrarugged service machines, would have defeated even these had it not been for the work he and Karmikel had done on them during their last free hours on-world. They had wanted to give their party the greatest possible mobility during the final stages of the evacuation, and that care was paying off now. Paying off for him.

The sense of relief faded almost as it was born. His goal was still very high, and he would have to drive through a veritable blizzard of ash and lapilli to reach it, that and maybe a lot more.

At least, his course was straight and would in itself be easy. There was no need to alter his route now for fear of disturbing the sensibilities of any residents.

His heart leaped painfully. There was another explosion, not muffled this time, but sharp and loud and-extended. Something had blown out.

One of the fumaroles!

A boiling, darkly red wall burst from it, no cloud of ash or pebbles, but rock, broken, aye, but the pieces were boulders, and some of them would crush the rover as easily as if it were made of paper if they struck it.

That would not happen except by the vilest chance, for he

had not yet come into line with its path, but neither was he free from all danger.

The Commando stopped. His nerve was not sufficient to keep him moving closer to that terrible burning thing tearing its way downslope, and so he sat watching it, numb with horror and awe.

It was moving fast, very fast, and nothing could stand before it. Trees snapped off at the ground. Boulders flew from their beds, some to ride with it, others, too heavy for that, either to resettle or to roll downward of their own accord.

The High Monastery lay before it. He watched in a kind of fascination as it swept down upon the closely clustered buildings, engulfed them.

For nearly a minute, nothing was visible but the avalanche itself, then it was past, and he was looking upon a scene of complete desolation.

The destruction was absolute. Scarcely two stones in any place stood one upon the other, and some of those buildings had been constructed with walls three or more feet thick.

Sogan shuddered at the power that had been revealed before him, but he rallied his courage.

He looked down upon the city. Nearly a third of it, that farthest from the port, was gone, shattered even as were the buildings above him, but he had realized that must come, whether in this manner or in some other, and so no sense of horror gripped him. He had heard the last starships, his and Jake's and the shuttlecraft, lift and knew that there was no one left in Strombolis to be hurt in its dying.

His thoughts turned to the unfortunate ones who had been concealed in the smoldering rubble that was his goal, and he once more started toward it. He knew in his heart that they were dead, that nothing could have survived the passing of that holocaust, but still, he felt compelled to confirm their destruction if he could. Maybe enough energy had been released to relieve the pressure long enough to allow him to come back down again . . .

Varn gripped the controls tightly and continued upward. He altered his course a little, for he could not bring himself to enter upon that path of destruction before he actually had to do so, but he would not permit himself any further swerving from his purpose. Until he could confirm their deaths, there was the shadow of a chance, opposite to all reason as it was, that one of the three might still be alive, burned, dying, perhaps, but living and in need of aid, if it be only that of granting the final grace.

He reached the ruined monastery at last and leaped from the rover as soon as he ascertained it was safe for him to do so.

The stone under his feet was decidedly hot, but it would not sear him through the defensive oversoles he had shown the foresight to pull on over his boots, and he gave no more attention to it as he looked about him.

Despair filled his heart. How in space was he going to find anyone in the midst of all this? Nothing remained. He could scarcely recognize the outlines of some of the buildings. Atmobombs wrought less injury than this to the places they annihilated.

He began to search, however, and in a short enough time to surprise him, he found what he sought.

They were lying together behind what had once been the wall of a garden, so that they had been only partly buried. None required any help from him.

The top of one's head had been sheared off, but it seemed to be the intense heat that had killed the other two, for they looked as if they had been reaching out to the first. All were badly burned, although, strangely, their robes were quite untouched.

The war prince gazed into their dead, distorted faces, and suddenly his eyes filled with tears all his will was powerless to block.

They were so young. He had been no older than this when he had first put on a cadet's uniform. —By every god in the Federation, why had he not been able to reach them in time to save them?

Varn, look out! Above you!

Islaen! He whirled at the call and then froze as he stared upslope, his eye involuntarily seeking what he knew had to be the cause of such overwhelming fear.

His heart beat fast. He was too near and the grade above was too steep for him to see the crest, but a ruddy glow was emanating from the hidden crater.

Even as he watched, it grew perceptibly brighter.

Varn! Varn, run! Now!

He raced for his machine, gained it.

There was nothing he could do here, and somehow, by some impossible, vicious chance, or more probably by her own choice, Islaen Connor was still in the city below. He had to get to her before the Dragon struck again!

There was another sharp explosion, and seconds afterward, bombs began to rain down, red-hot rock and blobs of semi-congealed magma. The rover was hit and hit again. Sogan could hear the sizzle of scorching metal and prayed fervently that nothing would come too near his fuel tanks.

Pain! Desperately, his mind reached out, groped for his consort's.

Nothing. The Noreenan was still alive. That much he did know, but she was no longer transmitting, whether by her own will or because she could no longer do so.

Grimly, he forced more and still more speed from the straining, wildly jerking rover. Nothing mattered now, nothing at all, except that Islaen was hurt, probably severely, somewhere in that doomed city.

The former Admiral forced himself to concentrate on the two brief calls he had received from her. They were the only clues he had as to where she might be.

Not quite. Reason could supply more. The Commando-Colonel had been at the planeting field, but logic would send her to the docks, to the place where the *Daber* was moored. There, she would have the choice of waiting for him or of coming up after him along the course he must follow. It was to that place that he must go to find her.

Varn had reached the city when the glow increased to the intensity of the rising of a very small sun.

He glanced in the rear viewing mirror and saw a sight that turned the life cold within him.

A great cloud was rising over the lip of the crater. Black, it was, but shot with lightning and bearing within itself its own dull red fires, the fires of the Empire's direst hell. It remained there, swelling, churning, boiling, until it towered fully thirteen thousand feet above the enraged volcano.

The man hit the controls, demanding the last shred of speed from his vehicle.

He knew it. By the great Spirit ruling space, he knew what that dread thing was. *Nuée ardente*, preflight Terrans had named it, a mass of superheated gas so heavy with incandescent ash that it could not rise and so powered by the forces ejecting it and those within its own self that nothing could halt or turn it, a wall of destruction hot enough to incinerate everything within its path.

There was no thought to his driving, no consideration for the ground over which he moved, only the absolute need to reach the docks and the *Daber* before the Dragon's deadly breath. Praise every god ruling Tambora of Pele that the previous avalanche had not touched and destroyed this part of Strombolis, blocking the way against him . . .

Sogan came within sight of the docks. He spotted Islaen at once. She was at the pier's edge, braced against a pillar and stiff with terror but unmoving. Terror or something else. The whole left side of her face was scarlet with blood.

The *Daber* was beside her, in the water and free.

He braked the rover and sprang from it. Varn stumbled but with a desperate effort regained his balance. If he went down now, he was lost. They were both lost.

The Arcturian ran toward his consort, but she did not turn as he thought she would or respond at all to his coming.

Was this already a dead woman? Had she in her last act of volition set what she had known would soon be her corpse up as a signal for him? Her injury looked severe enough to have killed her . . .

There was no time to waste. He caught the Noreenan and flung her into the boat even as he leaped aboard himself.

The oars were ready in their locks. He blessed the Colonel for that. If he had been forced to delay to set them now, neither of them would live long enough for him to use them.

The *nuée* was almost on them.

Sogan put the full of his skill and strength into his rowing. Their only hope was to get to one side of it, out of its path. There could be no outrunning it.

He would never make it! The glowing avalanche was too huge, covered too impossibly vast an area, and it was moving far too quickly for mere human muscle to outdistance it. Already, the air was growing hot!

The cave!

He pulled for it, knowing it represented their sole hope.

It was near, and he redoubled his efforts, grimly ignoring the debris once again falling all around, the ejecta of yet another explosion.

The dark mouth loomed before them. Another stroke, and they would be inside.

A violent blow drove Varn against the *Daber*'s rail. He retched with the burning agony in his right shoulder but somehow caught the oar again before it went overboard and gave the pull that sent them into the waiting shadows.

There could be no thought of rest, not yet.

Using his left hand, the man wrenched the rebreathers off himself and off his barely living companion and flung them as far as he could from their boat. If the air became too hot, the gases in them might explode, though how he could expect either of them to survive such heat . . .

He cast himself down on top of Islaen, covering her as best he might.

What would happen? Would the cloud fill this place, burn them as the young Ascetics had been burned? Would the water boil around them and they be broiled through the thin sides of their little craft? Would they be steamed within it?

Do not inhale when it comes, he commanded, not knowing whether the spark still living within her mind heard him.

There was no time for more. The darkness deepened, and he looked up, unable to resist his curiosity despite his mortal peril.

The burning cloud was passing over the cliff, down, and out across the surface of the sea.

He flattened again as the first blast of it shot into the cave, holding his breath as he did so.

The air above him was very hot, but not as intensely so as he had feared, and that trapped inside the tiny boat stayed cooler still.

It did not grow worse. Apparently, the enormous forces powering the *nuée* did not allow for much dispersal, and it was all directed outward toward the horizon. What little did wash back into the cave dropped heat fairly quickly once cut off from the main cloud, which would itself cool and lose strength as the water and air acted upon it.

Would he or the Commando-Colonel still be alive when its end finally came? Relatively mild though conditions in the cave might be when set against all they could have been, yet still, they were dire in themselves. His back was burning, particularly across the shoulders where it rose highest to meet the cloud, and the pain in the right one was well nigh beyond the enduring. It was broken, of course, and the bomb, though it had fortunately ricocheted off again after striking him, had remained in contact with his flesh long enough to sear it to the very bone.

He thought he felt the *Daber* move, as if she were rising, but dared not look up to see if the roof were drawing nearer.

He could not have done so. Fear and pain and the screaming of his air-starved lungs all combined to best him, and a deep blackness rose up from within him to envelop all his being.

TWENTY-TWO

WHEN AWARENESS RETURNED to Varn Tarl Sogan, the air was pleasantly cool and nearly free of ash.

He lifted his head to find the world bright beyond his shelter, the sky clear and glorious with Pele's smiling light.

Even that much motion set his body alight with agony, and he fell back again with a groan, striking against the Noreenan's still form.

Islaen!

A sickness worse than anything rending his flesh forced him to his knees. She had not moved or spoken since he had first sighted her standing on the dock.

There had been so much blood. His terror of the *nuée ardente* had blunted his consciousness of it then, but now the memory of it was a fear inside him as deep as that which he had felt for the Dragon's sending.

The woman was lying on her stomach, as he had maneuvered her after stripping the rebreather from her. As gently as he could working with one arm, he turned her onto her back, reaching out with his mind as he did so.

Varn's eyes closed. She still lived. Her breath came raggedly in a manner that chilled him, but for now, she was alive.

The pulse was very fast and irregular, the skin cold to the touch. When he raised her lids, he found the eyes rolled back, but one was perceptibly protuberant, the sign that fluid was building up behind it.

There might be other internal damage as well, to her lungs and airways, since she had not been able to hold her breath, but he lacked her ability to test for that. She was too deeply

173

unconscious herself for him to reach her at all, much less ask
her to exercise her talent on her own body.

It made no difference, he thought dully. She was failing
quickly enough from those hurts that he could see. The
bleeding had stopped, leaving her head and face caked with the
drying blood. The scalp was rent, clear to the skull, he saw,
and there had been much burning. One of the bombs must have
struck her fairly squarely.

The Commando-Captain reached for the oars. He nearly
fainted again under the lash of pain the unthinking action
brought upon him, and it was several minutes before he was
capable of coherent thought once more.

When he did rouse, it was into total despair.

Sogan looked helplessly into the woman's still, bloodied
face. She had readied the boat. She had waited for him,
standing as a beacon in the midst of those burning missiles so
that he should not miss the *Daber*'s docking place. She had
stood even after taking this dire wound.

It had been one already slain holding that post. His weakness
now assured her death . . .

The war prince gripped himself. An officer of the Arcturian
Empire knew better than to give panic any rein, whatever the
crisis.

Very well, he had forced calm on himself again, but to what
purpose? Cool mind or none, their situation remained the
same.

The small transceiver—he was quick to check that—that was
part of the vessel's equipment had been smashed during the
bombardment, and their little communicators were strictly
relatively short-distance, on-world instruments. If they could
not get outside onto the open sea where they could be seen,
they would be assumed slain.

Maybe the searchers had given up already. Islaen's still
fairly liquid blood told him that no very great amount of time
had probably passed since they had entered the cave, but the
cataclysm had been so enormous, so utterly overwhelming,
that their survival would not be expected.

If that were so, they were already finished. The Colonel
would very soon be dead, and he himself could perish from
lack of water or from the effects of his own injuries, which he

knew to be severe enough, before anyone returned to the island, much less came to this cave.

He groaned. They had to get out, yet he could not row. He could scarcely move at all.

The man lay his head against the railing. He would rest awhile. Perhaps he might be able to use one oar, partly to guide, partly to push them out by poling against the wall with it, but right now, he knew his strength was not sufficient even to begin the task.

His thoughts drifted. He remembered how Islaen had called to him . . .

Varn Tarl Sogan's mind snapped alert. When he had recognized the danger looming over Jade of Kuan Yin, he had been able to contact her telepathic fauna from near-space and give them warning of their peril. Bandit was even now orbiting somewhere above Tambora. If he could only reach her . . .

He shook his head. There had been a multitude almost beyond numbering of gurries and goldbeasts to receive his call, and even then he had been able to transmit it only with Islaen Connor's help and with Bandit acting as a catalyst. It was hopeless, ridiculous, even to imagine that he could get through to the gurry on his own, or that she would then be able to transmit enough of his message to her human companions to hasten and direct their return.

Varn looked down at the once-beautiful face of Islaen Connor. No greater need had ever been on him. Was he such a coward that he would not even strive to win this woman her life? She had given him his, aye, and many times over.

He set himself for the trial ahead. At least he knew intimately the mind with which he needed to join. That should work to their advantage now.

He forced every other thought out of his consciousness as he concentrated on the union he must achieve.

The Arcturian called again and again to the gurry as he pushed himself farther and still farther, ranging up through Tambora's blue sky, into her near-space where the stars shone steady and fair.

There!

It was a touch only, and the link broke again even as it formed.

Varn's lips drew back in the snarl of a savage creature in

battle for its very life. Literally flailing his flagging consciousness, he willed himself back into position, ignoring the enormous strain on every fiber of his being. He must succeed and succeed now. His strength was not the equal of this effort. A little more of it, and he would shatter utterly.

He did not have to wage this part of his fight alone. Bandit had received his initial touch in complete surprise, but she had quickly recognized him and recognized his weakness. No sooner had he slipped away than she had turned her own energies to seeking him. Once more, their minds met, but this time, she was ready, quiet and calm and fully prepared to help hold him with her until he could deliver his message.

The war prince made no delay once their minds joined.

We live . . . hurt . . . Islaen very near death . . . cave by port . . . hurry . . .

He could say no more before the contact between them broke again. The strain on him was too great for him to maintain it longer even with the gurry's aid, but he withdrew with the knowledge that he had accomplished his mission. The rest depended upon Bandit's ability to arouse and move those with her.

Jake Karmikel stared numbly at Tambora's image in the near-space viewer. Islaen and Sogan gone. Both of them.

He shook his head, trying to make himself believe it. They had been through so much, individually and as a unit, during the War and since. He just could not bring himself to accept that the deceptively lovely flame world glistening in the *Maid*'s near-space viewer had taken them down. Whatever reason said about the impossibility of anyone surviving what had happened on Strombolis' island, some voice within him kept insisting that no one had actually seen his comrades die.

He gripped himself hard to hold his control over himself. That was nonsense. It would have taken more than even Islaen Connor's and Varn Tarl Sogan's courage to withstand a volcano's hatred . . .

Jake's thoughts abruptly froze as a seemingly maddened Bandit flew at him. She whistled again and again as her tiny, needle-sharp claws closed over his hand and tugged it toward the instrument panel.

The Captain's breath caught. He hardly dared permit himself

to acknowledge the hope suddenly born within him. "Calm down, little girl," he told her softly. "You'll have to tell me what you want."

His voice was shaking slightly. How could he communicate, really talk to, the Jadite creature? They were not bonded, and their minds could not meet.

Perhaps a rudimentary exchange would suffice. It would have to suffice, he thought grimly. "Bandit, I'm going to ask you questions. Stay quiet now. Whistle once for aye, twice for no. Do you understand that?"

The gurry whistled once; although her little body was trembling with the intensity of the emotion on her, she waited silently for him to speak again.

"Have our comrades contacted you?" One whistle. He moistened his lips with his tongue. "They're alive, both of them?"

Again, a single whistle, but a whimper accompanied it that sent a chill through him. "Hurt? Both?" A whistle and a vigorous nod of her head. "Badly?" Again, the affirmative answer.

Karmikel braced himself. "They need our help and want us to come to them?" He scarcely had to ask that, but the next question was crucial. "Bandit, if we planet, can you find them?"

The vehemence of her reply threatened to shatter her hard-won control.

The man stroked her. "All right, little girl. You'll get your chance."

He set the transceiver for ship-to-ship on the *Moon*'s frequency.

"Bethe, are you alone on the bridge?" he asked as soon as the Commando-Sergeant acknowledged his call.

"No. Captain Zubin's here with me."

The Noreenan hesitated only a moment. "We've just received a-transmission from our comrades. They're alive but hurt. I'm taking the *Maid* down."

"Where are they?" she demanded.

"Don't know. The transmission broke off, but Bandit should be able to locate them once we get on-world."

"I'm planeting as well," she told him. "You'll need help. All the area around Strombolis has to be one stellar mess.

—Never mind that debris!" she snapped in response to the protest he started to make. "Zubin and the two Patrol lads can stay aboard if they want and lift fast again as soon as I'm off if things still look bad . . ."

"Like all the hells, we will!" the Malkite growled behind her.

Bethe went on without answering him. "Those are my friends down there, Jake Karmikel, and I'm going to have a full part in their rescue. If you're thinking to try to stop me, retreat fast, or you'll be wishing you were facing a crack Arcturian invasion company instead of this single Commando!"

The war prince lay down beside his companion, too exhausted to attempt anything more in their cause. If only Bandit could get rescuers here in time . . .

Once again, he sought with his mind, not into space this time but into a darkness stranger and deeper still. Although he could not be sure that the one he found was truly aware of him, he could feel her curl against him as if in happiness and trust, and he endeavored to hold her even as his arm held her rapidly failing body.

Stay, my Islaen, he whispered. *Try to stay. Help is coming to us. Only remain with me, or it will all be pointless.*

TWENTY-THREE

VARN KNOCKED AND entered the infirmary chamber upon receiving its occupant's permission to do so.

Islaen was fully dressed and was sitting in a visitor's chair drawn close to the window. She had been peering out before he had signaled his coming; this room overlooked Horus' titanic spaceport, and the view from it was both spectacular and ever-changing.

The man studied her closely. His injuries had healed quickly, but the Noreenan's head wound had been a different matter entirely. It had taken days of careful attention to overcome and rectify the effects of that, and even now her physicians were declaring it a miracle that she had survived long enough to ever begin treatment.

You look beautiful, he told her, *and well.*

That last was a bit of an exaggeration, for the Colonel was still pale and drawn, but a few days' rest and ease would see to that. Her body was sound at last.

The woman laughed. *I'm glad to hear you say that! Maybe you'll be good enough to tell those white-uniformed jailers to let me out of here, unless I'm being held captive for some reason.*

Nooo! Islaen had to get better!

Bandit flew from her place on Sogan's shoulder and perched on Islaen's knee. She peered anxiously into her human's face. *Islaen's head doesn't hurt anymore?*

"No, love," she said as she stroked the feathered head. "I'm fine now. —I missed you, though. A whole lot."

Yes!

The Arcturian drew up the second chair and sat down beside

179

her. *The medics agree with me. They are processing your release confirmation now.*

Good! I've been thinking quite a bit while I was lying here . . .

Do not try to go too fast! he warned sharply.

No fear of that with you and our other friends around, she replied in disgust. *You've all made a fine set of gaolers for me.*

Her words were light, but her eyes fixed sharply on him. She thought that he had sought that seat a little too eagerly, as if he still wearied very easily. *How is it with you?* she asked gently.

I am healed. Once my full strength comes back, I will be fine.

His eyes had fallen as he spoke, as if in guilt, and he looked away entirely when he finished.

Islaen Connor sighed in her heart, knowing she could guess fairly accurately what was troubling him, but the war prince recovered himself quickly and was smiling when he faced her again in the next moment. *These thoughts of yours, Colonel. I was not reading your mind just now, but something tells me that they involve all of us.*

Only in a sense. Her expression darkened. *I'm not going to rest easy until those Alpha Gary weapons have been restored or neutralized.*

Sogan stared at her. *That is a job for Navy Intelligence, Islaen Connor, not for four Commandos and a gurry.*

I know. She sighed. *I just worry about loose ends, that's all.*

This one is the Regulars' loose end, her consort declared firmly. *As for you, Colonel, you are not to tax yourself with such concerns, or you will find yourself confined here for another couple of weeks.*

Aye, Admiral, the Noreenan replied meekly.

A look of mischief came over her as she bent to tickle Bandit under her bill. *I understand we've acquired some rather vocal supporters,* she remarked casually.

What do you mean? Varn asked, allowing her to draw him into her trap.

Jake was here this morning. He tells me that Zubin of Malki is claiming that we're the bravest people in all the galaxy and declares that he'll fight anyone or everyone on Horus who tries to deny it. According to Jake, he's been singling you out for special mention.

Space!

The woman laughed merrily. *Poor Varn! Of all the men in the Federation to wind up with that particular honor guard . . .*

You are not being amusing, Colonel Connor, he growled with no feeling of ill humor. It would take even more than a company of Malkite followers to trouble him when he saw her like this, alive and merry, after having come so close to losing her entirely.

Islaen sobered even as she was speaking, however, and her eyes darkened a trifle. If Varn had not been aware of that, then he had not been in contact with any of the port personnel since planeting. Had the medics been holding him quiet as well? No one, including Sogan himself, would have told her he had been severely hurt while she had lain in danger. They would instead have carried on a play . . .

Are you sure you're all right, Varn?

Aye, he replied, puzzled over the sudden change in her.

He realized what was disturbing her and merely shook his head. *I have had too much to do to bother visiting the local bright spots.*

Are you trying to kill yourself? Islaen Connor demanded angrily. *After all you've been through . . .*

Easy on the drive, will you! Since when have any of Horus' delights been a draw for me? —How much time do you think I had left over for sporting around, anyway, after making our report to Admiral Sithe, giving the Fairest Maid *a proper check, and visiting you here?*

The former Admiral grinned suddenly. *Speaking of our commander, by the way, he informed me that facing erupting volcanoes does not come under the heading of a Commando's normal duty, and he has put both of us up for another citation, first class.*

Her brows raised. *We appear to be building our own galaxy. And our fortune. If we ever have the good sense to retire, my friend, we certainly won't be entering civilian life as paupers.*

Retire and live on Thorne? Bandit asked hopefully.

"Sorry, love," the woman laughed. "I don't think either of us is ready to pack it in and live on past glories just yet."

She glanced at the war prince. There were things that she wanted to know. Her doctors had put a moratorium on all serious news while she was under treatment, but that should no longer hold now that she was ready for release. *What's going to happen to them,* she asked, *to the people of Strombolis?*

They will return and rebuild. They are only waiting now for the all-clear to do so. After everything that has happened, I had no trouble in getting them full disaster compensation, so they will not lack the means to hasten the work.

Good. They deserve that. —The Dragon?

It will be well studied and monitored so that they will have warning if it ever threatens to wake again, and, of course, the rest of Tambora will be studied as well. The locals may not like giving way so much to off-worlders, but they lack the necessary skills themselves, and the near disaster at Strombolis is proof enough of the danger that exists and could strike anywhere, maybe the next time with terrible results. They are a stubborn people, but they are neither stupid nor suicidal.

Strombol?

The Commissar is in a stronger position than ever. Everyone respects him for putting aside pride and dislike to meet his people's need, and all admire him for the way he handled his part in the evacuation, as well they should. He has no fear of any revolution now. His popularity would preclude it even if his enemies retained any standing whatsoever.

And the Gray Abbot? she asked, her voice hardening.

The Arcturian shrugged. *He will go back home as well.*

He tried to kill you!

Or one of us, he agreed bitterly. *We may be certain about that and everyone else with us, but there is no way we could make the charge stick, not in your Federation courts.*

His eyes glittered with a cold satisfaction. *No matter. He is punished. Everyone among his own knows what he tried to do as well as we do. It is no false claim of theirs that violence in any form is truly repugnant to them, and the evil they see in his attempt is magnified many times over by the fact that he sacrificed those three boys to bait his trap.*

Sogan fell silent a moment as the image of their dead faces filled his memory. *Those fine, young lives just cast away . . .*

Varn . . .

The war prince looked up. *I am not blaming myself, my Islaen, but I wish mightily that I had learned of their peril sooner or that I could somehow have moved faster.*

We all share that wish.

He put the memory from him. *All Tamborans hold him fully responsible for those deaths. The boys were his charges and*

*should have been brought out even as the Commissar and Red
Abbot saw to those under their command. It is no light matter
anywhere to be ostracized from all meaningful contact with
one's fellows, much less there, where society is so close-knit
and no contacts beyond it are available.*

*Above all, he knows his brotherhood is doomed, and by the
very plan he as much hoped would restore its influence as slay
one of us.*

*The Grays have been slowly dying for centuries, and the two
monasteries were actually each half empty, with only historical
significance and tradition keeping them from merging years ago.
Now, whatever faith remaining in their tenets after so long under
the rule of the Commissars and the Red Abbots is just about gone,
and the Gray Ascetics should be a memory within this generation
or by the beginning of the next at the latest. He will be the last
Abbot of his kind to experience meaningful rule and a position of
importance outside his monastery walls, and he must live out his
life knowing that he is responsible for his community's ultimate
destruction. Even the final grace is denied him since suicide is
likened to violence against another in Tamboran estimate.*

He broke that ban once, Islaen remarked dryly, but she
continued more thoughtfully. *Their going is a good thing. Most
of the fear and hate should fade with them, even if off-worlders
will never be really welcomed on Tambora. At least the
remaining apart will be based on more logical choosing.*

Aye.

She looked down at the purring gurry. She did not want to
accuse Varn or load guilt on him, but this she had to learn as
well. *Bandit's powers are known?*

The former Admiral chuckled. *Rest easy on that score,
Colonel. Our comrades are far too adroit plotters to betray her.*

How . . .

Jake made sure he boarded the Daber *first and casually
draped his jacket over the transceiver to conceal the extent of
the damage it had taken, then dumped it overboard while Zubin
and the Yeomen were getting us back to the* Maid. *Bethe knew
what was going on, of course, and did her part to keep the
others busy at the appropriate moments.*

Very neat.

It was well handled, he agreed.

The Noreenan's eyes grew somber. Another danger hung

over her, the repercussions of the role fate had forced upon her. Honor, justice, even sanity should make any move against her inconceivable, yet where feeling ran very high . . . *Are any charges being brought against me?*

He shook his head emphatically. *None. Circumstances proved what you did to have been absolutely necessary, and you acted with Federation approval throughout all of it.*

A soft smile momentarily lightened his features. *Also, there is the fact that some of your actions were more likely to win you adoration than anger.*

Necessity favored me in that, Islaen Connor agreed. *Necessity and fortune.* She still praised Tambora's strange gods that she had been able to save Ruger Ecks.

She smiled at him. *You didn't do too badly on that score yourself.*

Anguish ripped through him, and he pulled his thoughts away from hers. "How?" the Arcturian demanded aloud in sudden bitterness. "Is it praiseworthy to nearly lure one's commander to her death on a failed rescue attempt?"

Her head snapped up. She was hurt as always when he abruptly shut her out of his mind like this, but now she was angry as well. She had known from the beginning of their relationship that the scars on Varn Tarl Sogan's back were the least of those he carried and that life with him would not always be easy. That, she accepted, but she was damned if she would put up with his sulking every time need demanded that she act in opposition to his wish and will.

Why are Islaen and Varn mad? Bandit asked in distress.

Islaen glanced down at her. "A command disagreement, love. I think you'd best find Jake and Bethe now while we discuss it."

Yes, Islaen!

The Commando-Colonel waited until she was gone before turning flashing eyes on her husband. "All right. What's gnawing you now?"

"I think you know full well," he responded coldly.

"Probably, but I do not intend to spend the rest of my life trying to guess and second-guess the cause of your moods."

The former Admiral shrugged. "Why did you not stay on the *Maid* where you were safe? I would not have been permitted to come to you had our positions been reversed, or I would not if I were fool enough to seek your permission to join you."

"The privilege of command," she snapped.

Islaen stopped herself. That had been an unworthy answer. Varn was angry with her because he was unhappy, wounded. He deserved better from her than this.

"I'm sorry. —My duty to the port and city was fulfilled, and I was free to try to help you. At the very worst, I didn't want you to die utterly alone."

His eyes fell, then raised again some seconds later. "Do you know what it did to me to see you lying there, covered with blood . . ."

"Aye!" The Noreenan's brows came together in a pain that suddenly swept away from her control. "Maybe I haven't suffered the awesome losses you have. My kin are alive and well, my own never betrayed me, but that does not mean I would be all but unaffected by your death!"

The woman spat out that last. She fought herself and brought her voice back under her command. "Do you think I love casually, Varn Tarl Sogan? Have you no conception at all of how much of myself I've given to you, how much of my being I've invested in you? I might be able to survive and function as a viable and useful member of Federation society without you, but can you imagine for one delirious moment that I have any desire to do so? Do you think I can bear any more than you to have what we've built together wrenched away from me or to live with ashes and a memory? —Can you really blame me for wanting to be beside you, in life or in death?"

Islaen Connor had come to her feet and walked to the door of the room. She stood there, her back to him, determined that she should not break before him.

Sogan reached her in a few strides. "May the Spirit of Space forgive me, Islaen. I have tried to be the husband to you that you deserve, but I have failed you in your every need. Even in this, I have been so concerned with my own fear that I have rarely, well-nigh never, fully considered yours."

He wanted to touch her but restrained himself when she gave him no response. He deserved none. "I once asked you if you wanted to be released from this union. More than ever, you have the right . . ."

She kept her face averted from him. "Haven't you heard anything I've been saying?"

"The Spirit ruling space knows, I do not want to surrender

you, but when I see the pain my callousness, my selfishness, has caused you, not once, but time after time, whatever I possess of honor requires that I offer you your release again."

"Varn, I want you and to be with you. You are worse than a fool if you do not know that by now."

He looked at her a moment, then drew a deep breath. "You are right in saying that we could not retire to planet-bound idleness, but we could still claim command of the merchant fleet Thorne wants to build. That would be worthy, demanding work."

Islaen's eyes fixed him sharply. "The military's your life!"

The war prince shook his head. "Your life and your fulfillment are mine. Our present situation is very similar to my old lifeway, and so I adapted fairly readily to it, but we are not irrevocably bound to any service, not if it is a source of anguish to you. Your Admiral Sithe has already assured us that he will get us our release whenever we want out."

She smiled tremulously. "I know. Provided we're willing to do a little work for him now and then."

"Aye. —Islaen?"

She shook her head. "I've been with the Navy my whole adult life, and what we're doing is so incredibly important. I don't want to break with it, not yet."

Her eyes dropped. "I'm commander of what's become the most elite troubleshooting unit in all the Federation's forces, and I have to place that fact before any other consideration. There are still times, though, when I can act as a friend or a woman, in accordance with my heart and need, as happened at the end on Tambora . . ." She looked up at him. "Am I never to do that, Varn? Were even Arcturian war leaders expected to be absolute automatons?"

"Was I that?" he demanded. "No one can deny his humanity entirely and function effectively long-term."

His voice thickened. "We are not talking about functioning. We are discussing you. Both of us."

Islaen came into his arms. She reached out tentatively to him, and when she found his mind open again and receptive to her, she allowed her love for him to flow out to him.

His answered it. Her eyes closed as she rested against him. No woman could ask more than this man, more than his love for her, his caring and tenderness, his deep joy in her. *We are all right, Varn Tarl Sogan*, she whispered. *As long as we're together, we always will be.*